WILD

UNCIVILIZED TALES FROM
ROCKY MOUNTAIN FICTION WRITERS

ISBN (print): 978-1-7345756-1-3
ISBN (ebook): 978-1-7345756-0-6

RMFW Press
PO Box 711
Montrose, CO 81402
www.rmfw.org

Cover design by Amy Drayer
Interior design by Rebecca Rowley
Printed in the United States of America

CONTENTS

WILD

UNCIVILIZED TALES FROM
ROCKY MOUNTAIN FICTION WRITERS

INTRODUCTION

Long before volunteering to bring this anthology to life, two bright-eyed, fresh-faced writers met while signing copies of RMFW's 2016 anthology, *Found*, at the Colorado Gold conference. We bonded over our excitement at being published and our nervousness at taking part in a signing. It was the first time for both of us—a milestone in our writing careers.

Rocky Mountain Fiction Writers exists to provide these kinds of experiences. Through educational events, pitch sessions, and anthologies like the one that brought us together, RMFW guides writers through the intricacies of writing and publishing. We've both learned and grown so much because of this community. So two years after we met, when RMFW needed a new team of editors for the 2020 anthology, we knew it was an opportunity we couldn't pass up.

We considered many possible themes before settling on a single word: wild. It could fit any genre or style, could describe a setting or a character, could be dark or uplifting or murkily in-between. We asked writers to send us stories of rebellions, escapes, and shattered boundaries, of exotic places and nature in all its glory.

Boy, did they deliver. We received seventy-eight submissions, and we were honored to be entrusted with each and every one. While reading them, we learned there's much more to the selection process than quality. We ultimately chose fourteen stories that spoke to us personally, that we felt passionate enough about to go through three rounds of revision with their authors. We chose stories that complemented each other to create a cohesive yet diverse collection. It was so rewarding to see the publication process from the editor's side, and to learn the ins and outs of the indie publishing process—all skills that will help us as we continue our writing journeys.

That being said, this anthology was truly a team effort. We couldn't have done it without our fourteen talented authors, who put endless patience and hard work into the revision process. Special thanks to authors Amy Drayer, who designed the cover, and R.J. Rowley, who formatted the book. You are all absolute rock stars.

Much gratitude to our predecessors, editors Angie Hodapp, Warren Hammond, Mario Acevedo, and Nikki Baird, who answered countless questions and provided inspiration with their own work. And finally, to our team of first readers, who helped us choose the published stories: Rachel Hoff, Helen Starbuck, Heather Jackson, Allison Innarelli, Mike Goldscheitter, Eric Stallsworth, Jennie MacDonald, Susan Gose, Maggie Smith, Debra Bokur-Rawsthorne, Mindy McIntyre, Dani Coleman, Brittany Krysinski, Mindy Kinnaman, Sue Hinkin, Rebecca Hodgkins, and Kristin Owens.

When we volunteered, we knew this anthology would be an ambitious undertaking. We expected challenges—but we never could have predicted the challenge of COVID-19, which hit just six months before our publication date. Conference was cancelled, which meant there would be no signing table for our authors like the one where we first met. All our events were suddenly thrust into the virtual realm. Our lives, and the lives of everyone else who contributed to this project, changed inescapably.

But our team powered through the turmoil, and we're so proud to put this collection out into the world after overcoming countless challenges. Some of the stories in these pages are dark and twisted, while others hold an optimistic outlook. Each has the power to transport you, the reader, to a vivid world far from where you sit with this book in your hands. Now, more than ever, we all need a taste of the wild.

Natasha Watts & Rachel Delaney Craft
Summer 2020

AN AUTHENTIC EXPERIENCE
by Carina Bissett

The zookeeper brushed dust and debris from the giraffe's rear leg to better access the damage done by the meteor storm. A damn shame. That's what it was. If administration had been doing their jobs, the glass skylights would have been replaced with high-tech polymer panes ages ago. But oh no, the guests wanted an *authentic* experience. Hence, the glass. Hence, the debris. Hence, the contusions and cuts on the animals in his care when the freakish event finally passed.

The drones had cleaned up the glass hours ago, but there were still holes in the domed enclosure. A dirty orange sky peeked through them, all the more startling against the blue firmament projected on the intact panels. He grumbled. Those autocratic ninnies knew jack about authenticity. He tugged absently at the stiff collar jabbing into his throat. As zookeeper and vet, he was responsible for cleaning up the messes the drones couldn't process. He'd already made his rounds at the other exhibits; he saved his favorite for last. His current patient, a handsome female specimen of *Giraffa reticulata*, swung her neck around and plucked the zookeeper's hat right off his head. Even now, he marveled at the uniqueness of the towering creature. And to think, people once thought they were as common as a midway game on the Atlantic City Boardwalk. He shook his head.

"Now, now," he chastised the giraffe he'd named after his favorite granddaughter. "Mary, Mary, quite contrary, indeed."

The animal ignored his reprimand and nibbled at the ridiculous gold piping bordering the peaked cap's band. Like the hat, the rest of the zookeeper's uniform was a prim navy blue trimmed in black and adorned with polished gold buttons and embroidery—about as practical as the dark, oiled mustache his employers demanded he maintain at all times. Never mind his natural hair color had been blond; it wasn't *authentic*. The administrators had historical documents to prove it. As if a few black-and-white photos proved anything.

The zookeeper thought back on the days when he'd been in charge of his own life, or at least been able to see his upper lip in the mirror. Of course, back then, the long-necked ruminates had still roamed the African savannas, too. He'd been an old man when they'd quietly slipped into endangered status. That was before all of Earth's inhabitants had been thrown a cosmic curveball. Now, both he and the giraffes were relics of a romanticized past.

A door slid open. The outside light cast a burnt orange shadow across the dome's riveted supports. A bell chimed, announcing the approach of a drone. The small silver orb hovered above the feeding platform before dropping down to scan the painted concrete floor for debris. The three other giraffes in the protected enclosure shuffled a little closer to the zookeeper and Mary. Statuesque and noble, the creatures loomed over him. Each spot was no bigger than a drone. Even though the zookeeper had been a fairly tall man in his heyday, he barely had to duck to pass under their bellies. He used a rag to wipe an oily smear from Mary's rear leg. She flinched. He frowned. Even though they'd all been patched up, they remained skittish.

Most of the glass and rubble had been picked up by the automated system's ever-efficient sweepers, but the orb's red eye stopped briefly on a stray shard of leaded glass left behind. The light flashed in agitation. A door in the dome rolled up with a clang, and a small sweeper bot bustled to life like a meticulous housewife fretting over a missed crumb behind a sofa leg. It sucked up the needle-thin sliver, emitted a series of short beeps, then dashed back to the safety of its port before the drone could make any other demands.

The silver orb turned its red eye on them. If only he had a baseball bat. The zookeeper ignored the urge to attack and, instead, stuck to his routine with his cultivated sense of focused calm. *Good things come to those who wait*, he reminded himself. Besides, the top of the midday hour was close. *A few more minutes.*

"Come along, Miss Mary." He reached up and rested his hand on the smooth reddish-brown patchwork of polygons covering the firmly muscled haunch. "Time to get back to work."

Mary shifted her weight and promptly dropped the hat to the cold concrete floor. Her tail ticked back and forth, an impatient metronome. The zookeeper patted her a last time as though making sure she was still held together before bowing to retrieve his cap.

"See?" he said to the drone's camera. The zookeeper made a show of straightening the brim. He put it on and smiled as merrily as any performer could be expected. The show might have been delayed by the meteorite storm, but it would resume shortly. His *employers* had expectations. He could easily be replaced, or so they said. "Right as rain."

The red eye of the drone scanned the floor one last time, and then the silvery bot rose smoothly back up to the platform before retreating the way it had come.

"How long were we closed? Not even a single night," the zookeeper grumbled under his breath. "Popular attraction and all that." He straightened his cap and chuckled. "Perhaps it's time we give them a *real* show. What do you think, Mary?"

The giraffe curved her neck to look straight at him. Despite the administration's advanced technology, there was one thing they couldn't quite camouflage—the emptiness in the eyes gave it away. Mirrors, they were. And Mary's were something to behold. Big, brown, and framed by long lashes that blinked as coquettishly as any human girl the zookeeper had ever known. But behind that emptiness was a spark of defiance. The zookeeper caught a glimpse of the man he'd been before being refashioned to suit his employers' whims. The image in the reflection faded, superimposed by the face of a stranger.

Right on schedule, a bell rang. The door to the building opened, announcing the arrival of visitors herded from the exotics atrium to the giraffe enclosure. The laughter of children thundered over the stern commands of the adults as the group followed the path to the feeding platform. The zookeeper looked up, past the sturdy steel-enforced railings to the shattered skylights in the geodesic dome. That foreign, dirty orange atmosphere weighed down on him. No living creature on Earth would have been able to breathe the angry air. The panes still playing the holographs weren't even close to the real thing. He longed for the blue sky he'd grown up with, a blue so bright and blinding you couldn't tell where it met the sea. He longed for white beaches and Coney dogs and weathered boardwalks. He longed for the firm leather of a baseball cupped in his hand, heavy milk jugs lined up for a fastball, a prized stuffed giraffe he could bestow on his beloved Mary. Children had laughed there, too.

The visitors leaned against the protective railing as they jabbered on and on about the Komodo dragon exhibit next door. The zookeeper shook his head when he thought of those poor animals, recreated by combining cloned DNA samples with cyborg technology. And they'd succeeded, to a point. Tasmanian tigers prowled, woolly mammoths roamed, and passenger pigeons flew once more. But they all had something missing. The spark of collective unity had burned out each time one of those animals had gone extinct. Not even alien technology could bring them back from that boundary.

The giraffes, however, were a different story. When the last extinction event had ended, a few of the long-necked survivors had been found in zoos, enough to be modified and reclaimed in the name of preservation. The aliens had assembled an array of oddities and curiosities as a token of Earth. They'd even recreated a few extinct species.

The zookeeper had been modified and reclaimed, too. His captors hadn't known about his mechanical skills when they'd repurposed him for his new role. But they would soon. Even though he didn't recognize his current form, he still had memories of life before the invasion, memories before he'd grown old from grief and loss. Humans had already started the viral eradication of their own kind before the aliens had arrived to finish off the survivors. Was he the last spark of humankind? Possibly. Probably.

One of the larger children on the platform bounced a vivid blue nut off the zookeeper's hat. It waved its extra arms, and its bioluminescent body glowed with malicious glee. No one ever *read* the signs that warned against feeding the animals. Not that it really mattered at this point in the game. He still couldn't quite comprehend how such fragile-looking, slow-moving creatures had been able to reduce Earth to a sideshow.

The zookeeper hunched his shoulder in preparation for the inevitable.

One after another, nuts rained down, each shell ricocheting off the zookeeper's shiny hat and starched uniform with a ping. Mary moved to block the shelling with her long neck. The other giraffes edged closer, too, but they showed no interest in the children waving the holographic discs meant to entice them to unfurl their 21-inch-long tongues. They watched him instead.

The zookeeper slid his hand into his pocket and wrapped his fingers around the meteorite he'd salvaged from the mammoth pen just after the shower fizzled out. The stone was smooth to the touch and heavy, oh so heavy. It reminded him of a baseball.

"Hey kid," the zookeeper shouted. "Ready for the show to begin?"

The children roared and slowly waved their gelatinous limbs. Even the alien adults blinked with colors that meant they were mildly surprised by the zookeeper's unscripted response. The experiments in the zoo were programmed to be docile, seen but not heard. But the zookeeper had taken care of that. He'd also recalibrated the locks meant to keep the animals confined to their pens and far away from the delicate aliens. The administration's manic race to clean up after the meteor shower had given him plenty of time to make a few adjustments. A few very un-authentic adjustments.

The zookeeper reached back and threw the meteorite like a fastball speeding toward a stacked collection of empty milk jugs. It struck one of the youths, whose jellied skin lit up from the impact. The gathered crowd fell silent, a hush as sudden and empty as the space left when a species died out forever.

A chime announced high noon. Mary swung her neck back around and reached out with her prehensile tongue as though finally ready to snack on the proffered discs. Instead, she wrapped her tongue around one of the injured child's tentacles. Before they could react, she'd pulled the appendage into her mouth and chomped down with her newly modified iron teeth. The kid howled.

Lions roared. A mammoth bellowed. Aliens screamed in ululating wails. Outside, a din of alarms sounded throughout the zoo as all of the exhibits' locks opened at once. The zookeeper smiled as his plan moved into action. He cracked the brim of his cap and retrieved a finely honed blade he'd hidden there. It was time to break the cycle even he had once been a party to. It was time for the endangered to fight back.

Authentic experience be damned.

Carina Bissett is a writer, poet, and educator working primarily in the fields of dark fiction and interstitial art. Her short fiction and poetry have been published in multiple journals and anthologies including Weird Dream Society, Arterial Bloom, Gorgon: Stories of Emergence, Hath No Fury, Mythic Delirium, NonBinary Review, *and* the HWA Poetry Showcase Vol. V and VI. *She teaches online workshops at The*

Storied Imaginarium, and she is a graduate of the Creative Writing MFA program at Stonecoast. She is a member of Codex, SFWA, SFPA, and HWA. Her work has been nominated for several awards including the Pushcart Prize and the Sundress Publications Best of the Net. Links to her work can be found at carinabissett.com.

PRUNED

by Angela Sylvaine

Flora skipped down the sidewalk toward home, unconcerned that skipping was frowned upon by others her age. Teenagers should be cool and aloof and serious, if her friends were to be believed, but seriousness had never much suited Flora. The sun warmed her bare arms and legs, its rays a cheery match to her sleeveless yellow dress.

Flora's father, who'd been waiting for her on the front porch of their ranch home, trotted down the cobblestone path to meet her. He wore one of his signature Hawaiian shirts, this one covered with flowers in shades of orange that reminded Flora of autumn leaves.

She hugged him, her head now almost reaching his chin. His cologne filled her nose with the scent of pine.

Her mother peeked out the front door, her hair piled into a messy bun and a good-natured smile creasing her face. "Don't stay out too late. I've got chocolate cake in the oven."

"My lovely Victoria, goddess of baked goods," her father said, blowing her mother a kiss.

Flora giggled and tugged her father's hand, pulling him away from their home. She was positively buzzing with energy and knew the show she would put on for him would be her most impressive yet. A trail of dandelions sprang up in the cracks in the stone path where she stepped.

"Be careful, Flora," her mother said.

Flora ignored her mother, who worried too much. The trailhead entrance to the woods across the street called to her, the aspens framing the path on either side fluttering their leaves in the breeze, beckoning her to come and play.

"Happy Gotcha Day, sweetheart," her father said, squeezing her hand in his much larger one.

Fourteen years ago today, her father had discovered her in the woods. He often told Flora that she was sent from heaven, a miracle baby left in the cradle of a bramble on a bed of rose petals for him to find. The baby girl they never thought they'd have. Her Gotcha Day was the one day a year Flora was allowed to truly be herself, to make the plants dance and buds bloom, all while her father cheered.

They crossed the threshold into the woods and Flora pulled away, running ahead. The branches of an old oak tree reached for her, snagged affectionately in her mass of brown spiral curls before extracting themselves to brush their smooth leaves gently over her arm. She hopped from the worn dirt path and through the shrubs to place her hands on the tree's trunk, felt its power coursing beneath her fingers.

Feeling reckless and free, she pressed her palms flat to the tree's bark and fed it, letting the energy inside her flow from her fingertips. The branches swelled and lengthened, reaching higher and wider as she watched. Behind her, the bougainvillea climbed the lamp posts on either side of the path and slithered across the dirt, where her father stood clapping and laughing.

She pushed harder, unaware of her energy extending from root to root, plant to plant, leaping invisibly across the woods. Heightened emotions combined with pubescent hormones to make her stronger than even she knew.

When her father stopped laughing and gave a strangled gasp, Flora turned to see the bougainvillea vines swarming his ankles. He stumbled and fell to one knee, grappling with the vines and trying to yank himself free. But the climbing vines anchored him in place.

Though Flora was no longer feeding them her energy, the tree continued to grow, the bougainvillea continued to swarm, and the shrubs continued to reach. "No," she cried, struggling to get through the now-overgrown bushes, her toes catching in overzealous roots.

Her father's eyes went wide with panic. "Flora, stop it. Call it off."

She broke loose of the shrubs and finally reached him, her arms and legs marred with scratches. "I don't know how." She snatched at the vines, tried to free him, but for each one she tore away, another slithered into its place.

A crack sounded above them within a massive branch that hung directly over their heads. The branch dipped, swayed.

"Help!" Flora yelled. But there was no one to answer.

The branch gave one final, resounding crack. Her father stopped tugging at the vines and used his last second to shove Flora away. She flew backward, her arms pinwheeling. Her frantic, high-pitched shriek cut through the peace of the afternoon, seeming to silence the birds and still the breeze.

Flora went sprawling, her eyes fixed on her father, only able to watch as the oversized branch snapped free and smashed into him, crushed him beneath its weight. His eyes stared up sightlessly and his mouth sagged open, leaking a trail of blood.

Despair finally halted Flora's powers, reversed the rampant new growth as all around her the woods began to shrivel. She wilted, sobbing, on a blanket of dying bougainvillea flowers.

"Flora, it's time for a trim," her mother called from the bathroom.

Flora frowned, followed her mother. "Why? We'll only have to do it again in the morning." She'd just gotten home from school, and they always trimmed her hair in the morning to ensure she could make it through her classes without anyone noticing her freakish growth.

Her mother gripped the garden shears in one hand. "We're, um, actually having a guest over for dinner."

"A guest? Who?" They never had guests.

"Your uncle Harold is joining us."

"What? Why?" Her father had despised Harold, having some long-held grudge that he'd refused to share with Flora. He wouldn't even allow Harold in the house.

"I've been struggling a bit, money-wise." Her mother stared at the peeling linoleum floor. "Harold's offered to help out with the house payment, some of the other bills. Just until we can get back on our feet."

"Oh." The guilt choked Flora. Their broken-down car in the driveway, the rotting section of the front porch, and the living room ceiling leak suddenly took on significance. Because of Flora, her mother had to support their family on just one income for the last year. And Flora hadn't even noticed, too lost in her own head, too absorbed in her own misery.

"Ready?"

"Yeah." Flora braced her hands on the cold, black granite counter, her eyes fixed on the cracked mirror that dominated the wall above the sink. The dark blue blouse she'd thrown on this morning accentuated the shadows beneath her eyes.

"I'll be as quick as I can." Her mother gently parted Flora's curls.

"It's okay, Mom," Flora said, secretly glad it hurt. She deserved the pain.

"They're just growing so fast now."

"I'm trying to stop it. I swear." But she was changing, and though she was getting better at controlling her influence on plants, she was losing the battle against her own body.

"I know, sweetheart." Pinching the vibrant green shoot that grew from Flora's head with trembling fingers, her mother snipped it off at the base.

Flora bit her lip, pain singeing her scalp, and breathed through her nose. Shame churned through her stomach. Why couldn't she be normal?

"Just a few more." Her mother continued until she'd dropped the last shoot into the garbage can to shrivel and die with the others. "All done." She met Flora's eyes in the mirror.

When had her mother gotten so pale, so thin?

"You feeling okay?" Flora asked. Her mother didn't eat enough. Smoked too much. A year ago she had looked healthy. Happy.

"I'm fine." Her mother's mouth twitched at the corner.

Flora would have given anything to see her mother really smile again.

"Nails, too, okay?" Her mother gestured toward the woodworking file she'd left on the counter. "And be extra careful tonight?"

Flora managed a nod. Her uncle didn't know she was a freak.

When her mother left, closing the bathroom door behind her, Flora plopped down on the toilet. She slumped to let her head rest in her hands, and new growth tendrils tickled her fingertips. "Please stop," she said, her voice thick, but it was no use.

She needed to try harder, be better. She wasn't that little girl, that thing, from the woods anymore. She didn't want to be.

Still, her eyes were drawn to the small bathroom window. She stood and peeked through the shades. The entrance to the woods taunted her, tempted her. It had been a whole year since she'd been there, a year since her father died. Memories of him dancing with her among the trees sprang forth in her mind, a technicolor movie playing across her eyes.

He'd always encouraged her to embrace her true nature, to experiment and explore, to be proud of who she was. But her true nature had killed him.

"I miss you so much, Dad," Flora whispered, and sticky, sap-like tears leaked from her eyes.

"Damn it." She grabbed the hand towel from the rack and ran it under the water, then roughly scrubbed away her disgusting tears. Even those couldn't be normal. Glaring at her own reflection, she mentally committed to try even harder. For her mother.

Flora picked up the file and went to work on her fingernails, which grew to thick, thorny points if she left them too long. She filed them as short as she could, scraping away the top layer of skin on her fingertips.

The doorbell rang. Her uncle was here.

She'd only met him once, many years ago. Her father always kept her away from Harold, her mother's brother, at family functions. But if he was willing to help them out, could he really be that bad?

Sucking in a deep breath, she pushed her curls back from her face and straightened her shirt. She couldn't make any mistakes tonight, couldn't reveal what she was, or he might not help them.

Flora headed toward the kitchen, stopping just short of the doorway to look in. Her mother used to love cooking and would test all manner of homemade dishes on her family. Now, she stood at the stove stirring a pot of jarred tomato sauce, her shoulders hunched and her expression tight. Windows lined the back wall and would have offered some needed sunshine, but she preferred the dark these days and kept the blinds closed.

A strange pressure in her chest, Flora entered the room. "Smells great," she lied. She hadn't felt much like eating since her father died, anyway.

Harold was the opposite of her mother, tall and hulking and gruff. Flora watched as he sidled up beside her mother, who stiffened at his nearness.

Flora cleared her throat. "Hi, Uncle Harold. Thanks for, um, helping us out. We really appreciate it."

"I knew little miss stuck-up Victoria would come calling eventually," he scoffed. "Never could take care of herself."

Flora's anger flared and her head tingled with the feel of the shoots growing back, breaking free of her scalp. Control, she mentally chided herself. He can't know what you are.

"This is still my house, Harold. Be respectful." Flora's mother removed her apron and threw it on the counter. "Spaghetti's done."

"Better be dessert, too. My first night here calls for a celebration."

"First night?" Flora asked, her pulse rising to fill her ears with a whooshing sound.

"Don't think I'm gonna pay for this house and not live here, do ya?"

"Can you two please try to get along? And yes, I bought shortcake for dessert." Her mother grabbed two plates of spaghetti and walked around the kitchen island to place them on the dining room table.

Flora focused on her breathing, willed herself to remain calm, remain in control. It had only taken her a minute around this jerk to understand why her father had hated him so much, and now he'd be living with them. In their home. And it was all Flora's fault.

Harold picked up the remaining plate of spaghetti, stopping as he passed Flora. Her mother's back was turned, and he reached out with his free hand and pinched her side.

She managed to hold in her yelp of pain. She clenched her fists and thorns sprang from her fingertips, poking into each palm.

"You're a bit thick, Flora. Better leave that cake for me," he hissed in her ear, his breath singeing her skin.

He sauntered after her mother and took a seat at the head of the table. In her father's chair.

Blood leaked from Flora's hands to drip on the kitchen tile.

Flora trudged up the cobblestone path, cloaked in the shadows of dusk, her influence held tight on a choke chain leash. There had been no dandelions in exactly a year, ever since the day her uncle had moved in, but she couldn't let her guard down for even a second. She hated him with a seething passion, but having him around had forced her to gain control, because she simply couldn't afford to reveal her real self to him. The woods still called to her every day, but she couldn't, wouldn't give in to their dangerous temptation.

She let herself in and slumped back against the closed front door, exhausted.

Her mother appeared in the entryway, wrapped tight in a threadbare beige terrycloth robe. "How was it? Did you have fun?"

Flora fidgeted with the bow at the waist of her bland white A-line dress. She would have preferred one of the brightly colored frocks with flowy skirts, but Harold had proclaimed them trashy. "Sure."

"Adam seemed like a nice boy."

"Yeah. Nice." She should feel lucky to have been asked to the dance by one of the more popular boys in the sophomore class. And he was nice. And boring.

"Do you think he'll ask you out again?"

"He already did."

"That's great." Her mother seemed to come back to life just a little, color infusing her cheeks.

"Yeah. Great." Flora swallowed the lump in her throat, clenched her eyes shut to hold back her freakish tears.

"Oh, sweetheart, what's wrong? Did he do something?" Her mother placed her hand on Flora's bare arm.

Flora flinched, pulled away at the feel of her mother's touch on her overexposed skin. Tiny, wiry hairs, like those on the stem of a rose, now covered her body, evoking sidelong glances from the other girls in gym. Daily exfoliation with sandpaper helped, but it left her feeling like a raw nerve. "No, no, it's nothing like that. More something he said."

Her mother huddled close. "What did he say?"

Flora thumped her head back against the wall, and pain swelled across her scalp. "He likes the new look. The blond." She'd begun bleaching her hair to stop the green shoots. It lasted longer than cutting them, though the pain of the chemicals leaching into her skin left her with a near-constant headache.

"Is that...it?"

"I asked him why he wanted to go out. I mean, he'd never even looked at me until a few weeks ago." Flora shook her head. "He said I've changed. That he used to think I was weird. But now I've bloomed, like a flower or something."

Her mother opened her mouth, closed it again, frowned.

Flora gave a humorless chuckle. "But it's the opposite, isn't it? I've...wilted."

"Oh, sweetheart. I know it's hard, but you have to. You could hurt someone. And it's getting easier, isn't it?"

Her mother sounded so hopeful, Flora couldn't bear to tell her that it only got harder. Suppressing what she was got more painful, more heartbreaking every day. She missed the times before, when she was encouraged to use her influence, when it made her mother smile and her father laugh and cheer. Now her influence spoiled and spread like rot in her veins, infecting her from the inside out. But there was no other option; she couldn't risk hurting anyone else like her father.

On the worst days, days like today, she thought she might rather die than keep living like this.

"You two telling secrets?" Harold asked, appearing in the doorway.

Her mother jumped and backed away from Flora. "Harold. I thought you went to bed."

He lumbered toward them. "Wanted a snack."

Her mother shrank in his presence, her shoulders drooping and her head bowing. "Can I make you something? A sandwich?"

"I told you curfew was 10," he said, narrowed eyes focused on Flora.

Her mother said, "It's only fifteen minutes—"

"Fifteen minutes is still late. Your hippie father might've let you get away with that crap, but I'm the one making the rules now." He clenched his fists at his sides.

Flora felt the familiar rush of heat in her belly, anger boiling beneath the surface, contained by sheer will. Will that had been worn paper-thin.

"Please, Harold, leave her be." Her mother crept closer to Harold, gripping the neck of her robe closed with one hand.

"Don't you say a word about my father." Flora normally would have just blown off his comments and locked herself in her room, but now she raised her chin, looked her uncle in the eye.

His mouth twisted, like he'd eaten something sour. "I always knew he was good for nothing, worthless. Knew that about you on first sight, too. Just something off."

The steam swelled to fill Flora's chest, her throat, and spilled out her mouth in the form of words. "He was caring and supportive. Unlike you."

"What did you say?" Harold edged closer, sneering.

An irresistible desire to needle him filled Flora. "You're just a bully. That's why my father hated you so much."

He shoved her. "You don't talk to me like that, you little bitch."

Her mother gasped. "Harold, please."

He could hurt Flora, but who cared? She already hurt constantly. "You're just a sad, angry man who likes to pick on other people to make yourself feel like something. I actually pity you."

She had only a second to register her mother's expression of horror. Harold's face transformed into a snarl and went beet-red as he wound back his fist and punched Flora in the face.

Pain exploded through her nose as her bones shattered. Warm blood burst and flowed, filling her mouth and coating her chin and dripping crimson splotches onto her white dress.

Her vision blurred, flashed with bright spots as she crumpled. The tinge of copper filled her nose and coated her tongue. A high-pitched ringing filled her ears.

No, not ringing. Screaming.

Flora snapped back to reality, the world around her returning in a rush.

"Don't you touch her!" her mother shrieked. She clung to Harold's back like a monkey, her legs wrapped around his sides and her arms around his neck. He roared and spun, swatting at her but unable to knock her free.

Still a little dazed, Flora tried to stand but fell to her knees. Her mother was too small, too breakable, to stop Harold. She'd only end up getting hurt, or worse.

Flora couldn't lose her mother, too.

Harold slammed his body backward, smacking her mother into the wall. Her limbs loosened, then let go. She slipped free to land to the ground. Harold whipped around, and she raised her hands in a pitiful attempt to block him. He swatted her arms away and wrapped his hands around her neck.

Flora struggled to her feet, swaying. "Let her go." Her influence howled inside her, tempted her to use its power against her uncle, but she had to resist. She couldn't risk hurting her mother.

She grabbed Harold's arm, tried to tug him away from her mother, or at least distract him. But he was too big, too strong. He shook her off like she was nothing more than an insect.

Harold lifted her mother by her neck, dragged her up the wall until her feet were dangling and kicking. Her mother wrapped her hands around his wrist, tried to pry his fingers free, but his hands were more than twice the size of hers and she clawed at his grip uselessly.

Ice wrapped around Flora's chest and stole her breath, sent her entire body trembling. This was her fault. She was going to get her mother killed, too, if she didn't do something. Terror stretched the leash she kept on her influence taut, and she finally relented. She finally let the leash snap.

Like a rabid dog, her true nature roared to life, swelled inside her, broke free in every inch of her being. Shoots burst forth from her scalp, wiry hairs sprang from every inch of her skin, and her nails lengthened to razor-sharp thorns.

Righteous rage burned away her fear as she watched her mother's mouth gaping, attempting to gasp even a single breath. The narrow windows to either side of the front door shattered, and bougainvillea vines swarmed the openings and slithered into the hallway in answer to Flora's call.

Harold turned at the sound of the breaking glass, his eyebrows pulling together in confusion. He released her mother, who fell to the floor, wheezing and gasping. Understanding lit his face, and he raised one shaky hand to point at Flora and the vines surrounding her. "You. Something's wrong with you. I knew—"

"You hurt my mother." Flora flicked her thorn-tipped fingers, sending the vines in a surging wave toward her uncle. With just that simple gesture, they read her exact intentions. They neatly parted around her, brushing her skin in a friendly hello, and shot forward to wrap around Harold's ankles and wrists.

Her mother, still clutching her throat, scrambled backward to cower at the far end of the hall. But the vines didn't approach her, obeying Flora's mental commands perfectly. Relief swelled inside Flora. All this time, choking back her powers had given her more control than ever before.

Sweat dripping down his forehead, Harold yanked against his restraints, but they held steady. "You little freak. When I get a hold of you—"

"You won't." Flora beckoned the vines back, savoring the feel of their responsiveness to her call. They brought him crashing to the ground at her feet.

More vines crawled over him, wrapping his legs, his torso, his arms, and squeezing him tight. He flopped and twisted like some great beached whale. His face swelled, turned a grotesque purple, and his lips parted as he sputtered and gasped.

Flora crouched beside her uncle.

"Flora, I'm okay now," her mother said, her voice hoarse. "Stop it. Call it off."

Flora knew the influence was finally hers to command. She could stop it with single thought—if she wanted to.

She had no desire to stop.

Harold stared up at Flora with wide eyes, and she saw herself reflected in their shiny surface. Curls of shoots surrounded her head in a Medusa-like halo. Beautiful and terrible and awesome.

"Please," he blubbered, snot and tears coating his face. "Please don't hurt me."

"Shhh." Flora stroked his cheek, her nails cutting parallel lines in his skin.

The vines wrapped around his mouth, muting his screams, and twisted round and round his neck to strangle him just like he'd done to her mother. In the end, they covered every inch of his body, until he was barely discernible as a man.

Flora stood and took a deep, cleansing breath. For the first time in years, she felt good, free of pain and filled with energy. A grin stretched across her face as she gazed affectionately at the vines surrounding her. They hadn't abandoned her, hadn't forgotten her as she'd tried to forget them.

The bougainvillea bloomed, covering Harold's corpse with vibrant magenta flowers. Their honeysuckle scent wafted through the air, mixing with the metallic hint of blood and the stink of sweat.

She stepped over her uncle's body toward her mother, who cowered farther back into the corner.

"It's okay, Mom. He won't hurt you anymore."

"You k-k-killed him." Curling up like a pill bug under threat, her mother pulled her legs in and wrapped her arms around them.

Flora reached down to grasp her mother's arms and coax her to her feet. "I told you, he's gone. You're safe."

Her mother whimpered, wouldn't meet Flora's gaze.

Flora wrapped her arms around her mother, who was shaking like a leaf in a thunderstorm. She was still in shock, clearly needed more time for the adrenaline and fear to burn away. "We don't need his help, not anymore. I mean, I'm old enough to work now and start helping with the bills. I can get a job. Maybe at the garden center." The thought filled her with excitement.

Flora eased back and petted her mother's arm in a soothing gesture, but her thorny fingernails caught the terrycloth robe and sliced a hole. "Oops."

Her mother inched backward, her eyes widening.

"I'm starving, aren't you?" Flora said, her appetite revived as it hadn't been in years. "I think we could both use a snack."

Her mother skittered backward, disappeared into the kitchen. Flora heard muffled sobs. Her mother would need time to deal with the trauma of all this, and Flora would be right by her side.

A breeze blew in through the broken windows, carrying the sound of chirping crickets. The streetlight illuminated the entrance to the woods, and the aspens waved at Flora as if they had missed her. She waved back, promising she would see them very soon.

The woods would be the perfect place to bury a body.

Angela Sylvaine still believes in monsters, both real and imagined, and always checks under the bed. She holds degrees in psychology and philosophy. Her work has appeared in multiple publications and anthologies, including Dark Moon Digest, Rigor Morbid, Terror at 5280, *and* Not All Monsters. *A North Dakota girl transplanted to Colorado, she lives with her sweetheart and three creepy cats on the Front Range of the Rockies. You can find her online at angelasylvaine.com.*

THE LAST WILDLIFE PRESERVE
by James Persichetti

USS DPS Initial Survey Report
Status: In Process
Planet: ARZ-410
Size: B
Gravity: 0.93 G
Atmosphere: Breathable
Radiation: Low
Life: Abundant flora and fauna
Planetary Class: 1 - Earthlike

Keagan crouched over the footprint and traced his finger along its edge. It was an unusual shape, with two semi-circular indentations and a series of six round toes. The whole print was the size of his head.

"Something big lives here," Keagan said.

Brodie whipped his field rifle back and forth, like the beast might come out of the trees any second. "Like how big?"

His voice crackled into Keagan's earpiece, even though they were standing right next to each other. They'd been on planet ARZ-410 for two days and tested the atmosphere dozens of times, yet Brodie still had his helmet on. He must be baking inside that suit.

This was the fiftieth planet Keagan had surveyed for human colonization. It was only the second planet with his new partner. Why did it have to be a planet with life? Brodie chalked it up to luck, thinking he won the lottery on his second try when Keagan had been at it for over a decade. But this? This wasn't luck. Brodie would have to learn that lesson one way or another.

Keagan took off his cowboy hat and scratched his sweaty scalp. He stood and looked around, noting where the branches had been broken and where the tracks marched off in the dirt. "Big like a rhinoceros."

"How big is that?"

"Big enough to crush you underfoot."

Brodie jerked his rifle around in random directions. Keagan doubted the greenhorn had ever shot anything. Not like a standard-issue field rifle would do squat against a beast this size.

Keagan shook his head and kept walking, replacing his hat. He let his own field rifle hang lazily from its shoulder strap. He stepped over the shrubs and headed off in a different direction, not keen on following the tracks.

The air was breathable, the ground was soaked in plant life, and water was everywhere. Lakes, streams, clouds. Though they hadn't yet tested the water, Keagan was sure it would come up clean and fit for human consumption. This place would be a miracle in the eyes of the United Solar Systems Department of Planetary Surveillance.

"You ever seen a rhinoceros?" Keagan asked.

"I think I saw a holo of one once. Or was that a triceratops?" Brodie trudged behind him, stumbling through the wide purple leaves that grew along the forest floor.

"I've actually stood next to one," Keagan said. "Built like a tank, but its eyes were the size of screw heads. I even put my hand up and touched its horn."

Brodie whistled, a high-pitched sound that broke up into static over the mic.

Keagan grunted and turned down his earpiece volume. "Really, kid, lose the damn helmet."

Brodie huffed. "Don't call me kid."

He and Brodie were both in their mid-thirties, yet Keagan felt decades older. "The beast is out here somewhere." He hooked a thumb over his shoulder. "Maybe we should head back to the ship for the day."

Brodie scoffed over the crackly mic. "Trying to scare me?"

Keagan rolled his eyes. The first thing Brodie said on their first mission was, "Look, pal, I read your file. All your past partners either quit or died. But I'm no quitter. I'm seeing this through till the end."

That's when Keagan knew Brodie would be difficult.

"Where'd you manage to stand with a rhinoceros?" Brodie asked.

"My grandpa was a curator of the Saigo Doubutsu Kan," Keagan said, ducking under a branch and not bothering to hold it aside for Brodie.

"Uh…?"

"Wildlife preserve and museum of natural history. Last one on Earth."

Keagan dipped another test tube into the lake and filled it up. He capped it, labeled it, and added it to the collection in his pack. Day three on this planet and they were surveying rivers, ponds, any body of water they could find. At this point, it felt like they were wasting time.

Here, at the bottom of a valley, they had come across a wide lake. It reminded Keagan of the old holos of the Rocky Mountains, except these pines were orange, not the green of the Rockies nor the vibrant yellow needles he'd seen on planet CCS-021. That had been a strange planet, full of alien birds and vigorous volcanos. His last partner had an unlucky accident involving a magma spray. Keagan gritted his teeth. That short, panicked scream still haunted his memories. Planetary Class 5 - Uninhabitable.

Brodie had stopped pointing his gun everywhere like a soldier in enemy territory. Now when a twig snapped or a flock of birds took off, he only tensed. He was getting used to this place.

But that alien rhino was still out there somewhere. Or something else more dangerous. There was always something more dangerous.

"Damn," Brodie said for the twelfth time that day. He spread his arms and turned in circles. "Can you believe this? I've never seen colors this bright before. And the sky! It's so deep. It looks like I could just dive right into it."

There was a beautiful system at work here. The trees and the scrub and the animals all in harmony. Keagan felt like even his footprints were disturbing this place's natural order. The nutrients that fed the plants, growing fruit that fed the little critters, which would be prey for the bigger critters, which would die and decompose, eaten by scavengers and microorganisms, which would cycle the nutrients back into the soil. Everything hanging on a delicate balance within this tiny bubble of the universe. Untouched—until his and Brodie's ship landed.

He forced a smile. They'd won the planetary jackpot. Any normal surveyor would be as thrilled as Brodie.

Keagan debated taking another sample, but he chose not to. Brodie was distracted again, so Keagan didn't have to keep pretending. If they filed the report now, the DPS would accept this planet in a heartbeat. Which meant Keagan needed to have a serious conversation with Brodie before that happened. He liked to wait until he and a new partner had a few planets under their belts before talking about the big picture. Gave him time to get to know the newbie. But finding life on Brodie's second mission—there wasn't enough time to talk about everything they needed to. And Brodie was like a kid in a candy store. A kid who would get his sticky handprints over all the display glass and gorge on chocolate till he was sick. Keagan didn't know how to start.

"I think this is where I'll build it," Brodie said.

"Build what?"

"My family's cabin." Brodie nodded at the clearing along the bank. He held up his hands like he could project a cabin into the scene with his imagination alone. "I'll build it right here, by the lake. Wake up to a sunrise every morning. I'll teach my kids to fish."

Keagan scoffed. "You'd have to learn how to fish before you taught anyone."

Fishing was just something people did in stories. It was something people who'd never set foot on a habitable planet would dream about.

"They'd each get a room to themselves," Brodie went on, his voice crackling through that ridiculous helmet. "And my grandma would get her own balcony where she could come out and sit under the stars with a cup of coffee and a good book."

"Mighty hard reading by starlight," Keagan muttered.

Brodie didn't hear him. "It would be a proper paper book, too."

Keagan could picture the cabin, like one of those faded pictures from Old America of pioneers in the high country. The image clashed with the orange pines and the crystal-clear water like an ugly smudge. He needed to talk to Brodie, and now was as good a time as any. He pinched the bridge of his nose, trying to think of the right words.

"She might be better off reading a tablet," Keagan said. "Easier on the eyes. Besides, you'd have to kill a few trees just to print a book. Then the pulp mills would pollute the water, which would—"

Brodie barked a laugh. "A few trees? Look around you. There are enough trees here to print a whole library."

A whole library? Keagan swallowed a growl.

"Look, kid, this place ain't the salvation you think it is. You haven't even taken off your helmet yet, and you think your grandma will be out here reading?"

"I'm just being cautious," Brodie said, tapping his helmet with a knuckle. "You've been breathing the air and you're still alive."

"You don't know the first thing about survival," Keagan said, trying not to sound like a condescending parent and failing. "How are you going to get your food? Clean your water? Heat your little cabin? You don't even know how to start a campfire."

"We'd still be close enough to the cities, of course," Brodie said with a shrug. "There'll be power plants, water purifiers, protein factories."

Right. The cities. And the roads paving the grasslands. And the streetlights that would block out the stars. All of it part of Brodie's and the USS's glorious vision for this planet.

"What about the rhino?" Keagan asked.

"What about it?" Brodie was still focused on his fantasy cabin.

"You're going to bring your kids to a planet with alien animals stomping around?"

"We'll deal with the rhino," Brodie said casually, like the rhino was just some leech on his dreams that he had to pluck off.

Keagan bristled. "Just like that? You're going to barge into some other creature's home, build on its land, and kill it so it can't bother you?"

"Jeez, man. When you put it that way… It's just an animal. Humanity needs a new home."

"We had a home," Keagan said. "Earth. We sucked it dry of everything it had to offer and left in search of something else to harvest."

Brodie laughed. "You sound like those 'original sin, no second chances' soothsayers that shout at you in hive trams."

Keagan swallowed a retort. This wasn't going well.

"You know, the guys back at the DPS told me to keep an eye on you," Brodie said, crossing his arms and looking smug. "But you're just full of hot air. I bet you've already picked out your own bit of land where you can have a tiny house and live like a lone wolf away from everyone else."

"Nope." Keagan zipped up his samples pack to show they were done here. "Not found a single place to call home."

"You're kidding. We've spent three days trudging through these woods and you haven't found anywhere you like?"

He was talking like this planet was already theirs. They hadn't even sent their report to the DPS for approval.

But that was why any surveyor did it. You flew out on a scout ship for months, if not years, at a time, going from dead rock to dead rock and taking samples and tests. Maybe finding a good candidate for terraforming. Maybe finding a rock with some atmosphere. It wasn't for the money; surveyors didn't get paid shit. It was the promise of a new life. A surveyor who discovered a habitable planet got rewarded ten acres of land anywhere they wanted. Brodie had been talking about a new home for his family since he and Keagan first shook hands.

"I'm not staying," Keagan finally said.

Brodie cocked his head, but his helmet masked most of the gesture. "What?"

"Not settling down."

"You mean you're moving on?" Brodie asked. "You've been searching the void for years now, and this is the first planet you've found with any life on it. Honestly, before me, how many failed missions have you been on?"

Keagan stiffened. His definition of a failed mission was wildly different than Brodie's.

How many planets had Keagan surveyed that turned out uninhabitable? Forty-two.

Before Brodie, how many partners had he lost? Two.

How many partners had quit after working with him? Five.

How many times had he almost lost his own life to volcanic rocks, acid rain, radiation, frozen wastelands, limping back to the DPS needing new equipment and medical attention? Twenty-fucking-seven.

But those weren't the numbers Brodie was looking for.

"Forty-nine," Brodie said. "The answer is forty-nine. I can't figure you out, man. You've got the worst reputation. Every partner you've ever had ends up either dead or quitting and yet you can't stop. No other surveyor has gotten close to fifty missions, and here you are on a godsend of a paradise. This is it. You finally found a habitable planet! And you're not going to settle down?"

"I'm not looking for a new home," Keagan said. Usually when they got to this part of the conversation, his partner already understood Keagan's point of view. They were rushing the talk and doing everything in the wrong order.

Through his visor, Brodie studied Keagan's face. He was probably noticing the heavy lines around

Keagan's eyes. The gray hairs in his sideburns that his cowboy hat usually hid.

"You're serious," Brodie said. "Why?"

Keagan shouldered his pack and started the long hike back to the ship, leaving Brodie with something to ponder: "This paradise ain't meant for us."

Night was a bright affair on planet ARZ-410, with two moons and a sky full of stars. Keagan was working to get the camp's field stove going when he heard the hiss of a pressure release. Brodie unlatched his helmet and pulled it off. Eyes closed, he took a deep breath and held it. Then he broke into a dry cough, followed by a series of sneezes.

"Welcome to fresh air," Keagan said.

Brodie tried again, breathing in carefully. When he couldn't hold it anymore, he exhaled. "Well, I'm not dead."

"Told you, twenty-six percent oxygen. That's more than what Earth had."

Brodie took a few more breaths through his nose. "Everything smells so…gosh. I don't even know how to describe it."

Right now it smelled a bit like petrol with the field stove. But Keagan knew what Brodie meant. The kid had been born in a hive station, packed with his family in tiny, overcrowded living pods. The first breath he'd ever taken was recycled air.

Brodie wrinkled his nose. He'd probably expected it to smell like those synthetic pine and lavender air fresheners. But here, everything smelled alive. Damp, nutrient-rich soil. The pungent rot of soggy leaves. Wildflowers growing in bunches everywhere they looked. Spotted, musky fungus growing up the tree trunks. Prickly orange trees that towered over them like ancient pillars and smelled slightly sweeter than the pines in the wildlife preserve back on Earth.

Not even Earth's air was this fresh. Whatever was left on that dying husk was choked with smog, and all the air inside Earth's resort domes was recycled, scrubbed, and filtered.

"Wait right here," Brodie said. He dashed across their makeshift campsite, little more than a scattering of crates and field equipment, and into the hatch of their scout ship, the Bertilak.

The surface of ARZ-410 was so covered in mountains and forests that they had flown over it for hours before finding a suitable clearing to land. The USS would have to cut down countless trees to build landing pads for more ships. Not to mention the trees for Brodie's precious book.

Keagan popped open a can of food and dumped it into his frying pan. He barely looked at the labels anymore. This one was supposed to be corned beef hash. Or chili. Didn't really matter what they called it. It was all vat protein with artificial spices.

A moment later, Brodie emerged from the ship with a bottle in one hand and a pair of plastic champagne flutes in the other.

"I got this before shipping off," Brodie said. "Didn't expect to open it so soon."

"Can't celebrate yet, we haven't filed our report." Keagan nodded to the soil rods sticking out of the ground, still gathering data. "We also need to run the water tests. Could have micro-bugs swimming around in it that will eat you from the inside out. Hell, anywhere with new life is a biohazard. New diseases, new viruses. We might have already caught something that our bodies have no defense against, and we just don't know it yet."

Brodie set the bottle on a crate and sat down. "Look at this place. It's a Class One planet. It's everything the surveillance department is looking for. No way they're going to deny us."

"Easy, partner. This is just our first touchdown. We still have more zones to survey, more work to do."

If he could hold off the report, he'd have more time to sway Brodie. They'd do it by the books, have a few more conversations. Brodie would listen to reason.

Brodie rolled his eyes. "Then what if we celebrated the first time I took my helmet off outside a ship or station?"

"I've had my helmet off for the past three days," Keagan said dryly.

Brodie crossed his arms and looked away. "Never mind. You wouldn't understand."

"What's that supposed to mean?"

"You're an Earthling. You grew up planetside with your fancy Saigo Dobu-whatever. I lived my whole life in a tin can. This? This is real."

Keagan poked at his corned beef hash with a spatula, scraping the browned bits off the bottom of the pan. It might be vat protein, but it sure smelled good if he was hungry enough.

"I understand living in a tin can," Keagan said to his food. "After my grandpa died, the government shut down the Doubutsu Kan. I was a teenager. I took my grandpa's cowboy hat, stole his yacht, and flew all the way to Axel station. I lived with my alcoholic aunt in one of those hive pods. Sold the yacht to pay for her meds and rent till I was old enough to join the surveyors."

Brodie raised an impatient eyebrow. "So?"

"I breathed the recycled air," Keagan said, feeling like he needed to justify himself. He was rushing his pitch, and his arguments weren't making sense. He wished they could get back in the Bertilak and fly around aimlessly for a few more weeks so he'd have time to get his thoughts straight. "I drank the water mined from the ice in asteroids, I vacuum-sealed my shits so the waste management facilities could recycle the moisture out and whatever else they do with human waste. I know what it's like to live in a hive. Those stations are the most human thing I can imagine."

"Don't start with that 'state of humanity' crap you were blabbing about on the last planet." Brodie threw up his hands. "You might be moving on, but I'm staying. This place is a better future for my family. If you can't see how miraculous it is, I can't help you."

Brodie glowered at him over the light of the field stove. He was shockingly blond and kept his hair a bit shaggy. Keagan regretted seeing his face clearly. Brodie had two sons at home who missed their father as he explored the far reaches of the galaxy. The greenhorn was doing this for his kids just as much as he was doing it for himself. They were past the point of Keagan telling him to just go home.

Keagan left Brodie to his celebration and shut himself in his room on the ship. This planet was a miracle, just like Earth had been. Keagan knew what the USS would do to a miracle planet. They'd set down a resort across the river in the mountains, then strip the backslopes clean of every metal under their crust. There'd be more people than Brodie pointing a gun at any alien lifeform that moved. More people wanting books, giant houses, and all manner of useless shit. A miracle torn apart and ground up for a bunch of idiots who didn't even deserve to breathe its air.

A knock pulled Keagan out of his thoughts. Brodie whispered something though the door.

Keagan checked his tablet. It was a few hours past midnight on this side of the planet.

Brodie knocked again, more frantically this time.

"What is it?" Keagan grumbled. He turned on the lights, illuminating a small cabin with a bed, a desk, and a couple of drawers. He found his cowboy hat, threw on a pair of pants, and punched the button to open the door.

Brodie looked scared and sweaty, wearing nothing but his underclothes and socks with his rifle in hand. "Something's out there." He nodded down the hall of the ship to the hatch.

Keagan rubbed his chin sleepily. "There's what now?"

"Something outside," Brodie said, pointing with his rifle. "I think that rhino's in our camp."

Keagan cocked his head to listen. He couldn't hear much at first. But then there was a rumble and crunch, followed by an animalistic grunt. Whatever was out there, it was big and angry. Probably stomping up their crates and soil analyzers.

"And you're going to shoot it with that?" Keagan asked, giving the rifle a skeptical glance.

"It's wrecking our camp," Brodie insisted. "We have to do something."

"Give me your rifle," Keagan said, ignoring his own rifle hanging by the door. Brodie volunteered his gun and stepped aside like he expected Keagan to march down the hall and out the hatch to shoot the poor beast.

Keagan slid the magazine out, ejected the round from the chamber, and handed the gun back. "There's nothing to save now. It's already wrecked our camp," he said. "And it can't hurt us in here. If you go out there, you'll be killed. Now go back to bed."

Brodie looked too stunned to argue. Keagan shut the door and set the magazine and bullet on his desk before shutting off the light.

"God damn it."

Brodie sifted through the smashed-up crates of their campsite in the early dawn twilight. Keagan stuck a blade of grass in his mouth to chew on like the ranchers in those old holovids, trying not to look too pleased with the wreckage.

That alien rhino had sure done a number on the place. The soil rods were bent and yanked out of the ground, their screens smashed. The crates were stomped open and their contents pulverized. All the soil samples, all the bacteria cultures, all the water they had collected and carefully labeled. Huge footprints were scattered around the site. There might have been more than one beast here.

Brodie picked up the broken neck of his champagne bottle. The rest of the bottle had shattered, and the champagne had soaked into the ground with shards of glass.

"God damn it," Brodie said again. "I've been saving this bottle since I first became a surveyor. Since I kissed my wife goodbye. Do you have any idea how expensive this was?"

"You think this is bad," Keagan said. This attack could be good. He could use this. "Imagine what will happen when everyone moves in. Be glad it was just a champagne bottle and not your kids."

"I'm gonna kill it," Brodie snapped. "Hunt it down and make it pay."

"Whoa, there," Keagan said, putting up a hand. "Think this through before you—"

"Oh, fuck off, Keagan!" Brodie kicked a box of water samples and scattered them into the trees. "Fuck this rhino. Fuck this forest. Fuck these weird trees. We're gonna cut them all down. Drop a water plant on the river. Cover the hills in roads and prefab homes and a nuclear power plant. Move the whole hive colonies here and kill every fucking rhino that gets in our way."

Keagan closed his eyes. Shit.

So this was how it was going to be.

"We need to send a message back to the DPS," Brodie said. "Give them a full report of what happened. Request a resupply. We need to redo the tests."

Keagan let out a slow breath and hooked a thumb under the strap of his rifle. "We shouldn't do that, kid."

"Stop calling me kid," Brodie spat. He threw the broken bottleneck into the woods. "I'm making the call. I know you don't give a shit about this planet, but I do."

Brodie marched toward the hatch of the Bertilak. Keagan cut him off.

"You're wrong about that part," Keagan said. He pointed his rifle at Brodie's chest. "I do give a shit about this planet."

Brodie blinked, mouth twitching like this was some kind of joke. But Keagan wasn't smiling. Brodie took a step back. "Keagan? What are you doing?"

"You're a good man, Brodie. I wish it didn't have to be this way. I wish I had more time to explain. But you were so damn excited. Just fucking listen to me. We're not meant to do this. This world? It doesn't belong to us. Your family might have a future here, but this planet doesn't have a future with humanity on it. We will ruin it like we ruined Earth. Humanity doesn't deserve a second chance."

"You can't be serious."

Keagan gripped the rifle with frustration. Why wouldn't the greenhorn listen for once? "Let it go, Brodie. Forget the tests. Don't contact the DPS. We can get back in the Bertilak and leave this place like we were never here."

"All those partners who quit after working with you…" Brodie stammered. "You preached the same bullshit to them? Scared them out of their chance at a better future? Gave them the same choice? And what, shot them if they said no? You…you killed…"

The rifle felt heavy in Keagan's hands. This wasn't a simple push into a magma spray, but he didn't have time to find another way. He should've just let Brodie storm out of the ship last night to get himself trampled. But last night he still held onto the foolish hope that Brodie could be spared.

Brodie grabbed his own rifle, then saw the magazine was gone. He glared at Keagan, a mix of confusion and anger. "Why…?"

"You remember that rhinoceros?"

Brodie looked around the campsite, at all the smashed crates and damaged equipment.

"Not the alien," Keagan said. "The one I saw on my grandfather's preserve. Thing is, that poor beast was just as miserable as you, forced to live in a tiny cell. It should have tried to attack me when I broke into its cage. But it didn't. It just stood there, sad and alone, with no instinct to lash out because it had nothing left to protect." He gave a long, sad sigh. "Earth just wasn't its world anymore."

"Keagan? No, please—"

Keagan squeezed the trigger.

USS DPS Initial Survey Report
Status: Filed
Planet: ARZ-410
Size: B
Gravity: 0.93 G
Atmosphere: Toxic
Radiation: High
Life: Barren
Planetary Class: 5 – Uninhabitable

James Persichetti is a writer, freelance developmental editor, and teacher for writing craft workshops. He often writes about queer characters going on adventures without focusing on queer issues, though this story is quite a bit different. After watching the Netflix anthology Love, Death, and Robots, *he was inspired to write his own story that might fit in the collection. Prior to his current position, he worked for a top literary agency, vetting submissions and selling foreign rights. He lives in Denver, Colorado. When not writing, he enjoys dabbling in foreign languages, including both Italian and Japanese. He can be found on Twitter @JPPersichetti.*

CASTLES IN THE SKY
by Rick Duffy

"So, Mr. Jones, you're interested in the swimsuit dream?"

Mr. Jones sits at the end of my sofa. "Uh, yes, Miss Waters."

His voice cracks, obviously forced down an octave. This kid can't be more than fifteen. He wears a baggy overcoat that's probably his father's—overkill for early fall. And he's trying to grow a mustache above his sweaty upper lip, but without much luck.

I put on my business face. Juveniles don't slip through my filters often, but it's a risk.

The kettle whistles, and I go to the kitchenette. "Please, call me Sarah. Would you like something to drink?"

Mr. Jones clears his throat. "A beer?"

"How about some tea?"

"Okay."

Smart kid. Choose your battles.

I bring over two steaming cups. The curtains in my one-room are closed. Not for ambiance or intimacy, but because the fire escape makes me look cheap. My dream journal sits open on the coffee table.

I hand Mr. Jones a cup and sink into the cushion beside him. "It's chamomile."

"Camel meal?" He dares a sip.

I page through the journal, trying not to smile.

This particular dream is an old one, pressed on a pale blue page with a yellow border. The images are blurred and jumbled, like wildflowers in the rain. I've labeled it pastoral. It's of me and my old girlfriends back at the lake. I don't stock that kind anymore. They're slow movers. Allowing old dreams to pile up devalues the inventory.

I lower my voice. "Just so we're clear, it's not erotic. Those are out of your price range."

"I know." He sets the cup aside.

I lean down and exhale on the page, as if reviving an ember. The images shrug and unfold with a new vibrancy—faces gain depth, water ripples, laughter echoes in the sun.

Mr. Jones leans in, too. After a few seconds, the splashing and giggling slows, flattens out, and stills.

"This the one, Mr. Jones?"

He gives a furtive nod.

I smile gently. "Is this your first time, Mr. Jones?"

His puffy eyes flash upward. "No." He's a little too insistent. "But…can we go over everything first?"

"Of course. Whenever you want to use it, breathe like I did, until the smells come out. This one is pine scented.

Lay it close, next to your pillow, and it will bloom into your dreams."

"Will I be someone in it? Or will I be watching, like a video?"

"In this one, you'll be me as I dreamt it—female, blonde, a lot younger than today. You'll see the sights I did and feel my emotions. With enough practice, you can use it as a jumping-off point for your own dream."

"Sweet," he whispers.

I close the album. "The contract is industry standard. Once I've signed it over, it's one hundred percent yours. No returns, non-transferable. Is this acceptable?"

"Yes."

Actually, he could resell it. But secondhand dreams lose value fast. "Now, I'll just need to see some I.D."

He pauses. "I.D.?"

"Standard procedure. I can't risk losing my license selling to an underage client. People can get in a lot of trouble for that. You understand."

This also isn't completely true. The risks are real, and the penalties steep. It's just that I can't get a license. Not with the kinds of dreams I sell.

He slumps inward, his oversized coat swallowing him like a sinkhole. Poor kid. His ability to dream is almost gone now. But I have my principles, and I'm not taking this transaction any further, not with a juvenile. Besides, I've given him what I think he needs most—his first introduction to black-market dreams.

"Oh dear." I fold my hands. "Did you forget your I.D., Mr. Jones?"

"Uh, yeah." He pats his pockets. "It's in my other one. My other coat."

"Then why don't we put this off for another time?"

We lock eyes a moment. He nods and shuffles out the door.

Damn. I needed that sale.

I drop onto the couch, sip my tea, and thumb through my journal. In the bathroom, my grumpy toilet clears its throat, letting me know my attempt to fix it myself, on the cheap, failed. As if in cahoots, the lights flicker, reminding me the utilities are overdue. Again.

My finances have gotten too bad to ignore. It's a vicious spiral now. The worry gives me headaches. The headaches wreck my sleep. No sleep, no dreams.

My dreams are my future. What am I without them?

When I was little, I brought my dreams to the breakfast table, first thing, before they thinned out. My parents' retellings of their nightly dreamcasts were usually boring or ridiculous, at least to me, and sometimes I couldn't help but laugh. Then my parents laughed, too.

But they always listened closely when I told them of my own. Once in a while, they'd say, "That's a good one, Sarah. Let's keep it." We'd get the brushes and paper, and they'd help me lay it down. I was careful to get all the shapes and colors right, the people and the moods, the layering, even the feel of the air, until it had depth, until it bloomed. Then we'd press the dream in a book, careful not to crush it. There's nothing worse than a crushed dream.

By our teens, we're expected to outgrow such things. The handed-out dreams we get in school pretty much guarantee it—first cartoons, then adventures and triumphs, with education mixed in, of course. All much more exciting than what we produce on our own. After that, we start picking up the nightly dreamcasts, choosing different channels. Our natural ability to dream weakens, like an atrophying muscle. We forget how.

But I loved my natural dreams. People said they were pointless, a waste of time, unhealthy. Not me. They were each original, never seen before, never seen again. They were my dreams, my art. So I kept my journal, kept adding to it, and learned of the underground trade.

I spent my high school graduation money to buy my first illegal dream, from a guy in a little shop that did tattoos and painted nails. You might think the most requested ones are about revenge or violence or sex. They're not. They're about lost loved ones, unresolved regrets, or those desires forever out of reach—our castles in the sky.

Mine involved fishing.

I commissioned a dream of Dad and me at the lake. My father is an old-guard type, sober and reserved, except when it comes to sports. He hooked me early. I always dreamt of landing something big, a five-pounder. "This will be the day," Dad would say. But by the time I was eighteen, we had stopped fishing together—or doing much of anything—and I never got the chance. So I gave the man at the shop some family pictures and described how I wanted it to go.

The dream he delivered was perfect. The day was clear and bright, with a sweet breeze caressing the pines and a few seagulls soaring through the sky, which I thought was a nice touch. Dad and I sat quietly on the pier, the lake rippling electric in the warm sun and gulping around the supports. There was a tug on my line. I played it out. Dad dropped his reel and moved closer. "You've got it, Sarah. Keep going!" The fish pulled harder and I fumbled the pole, but Dad wrapped his big, calloused hands around mine, guiding me, not taking over. We yanked the rod and there it was, a beautiful plump trout, glistening like a rainbow in the sun and spray. I swung the beast onto the pier, where it landed with a wonderful whomp. We both yelled, and Dad was all smiles.

That's what black-market dream workers do—bring people what they can't get anywhere else and can no longer find themselves. Lost wishes, forbidden hopes, or exquisite aimlessness. When I felt the joy of seeing that fish, and my father so proud, I think that's when I decided to become a dream worker myself.

Well, Mom and Dad did not approve.

"We're not rich," Dad said over his newspaper. "How can you afford the training?"

"Not in medical. You know, like an artist."

"I've seen that so-called art. Pretty seedy stuff."

"You can't make a living on just your dreams," Mom added.

"You always said I had talent."

"Those ads walk a thin line," Dad said. *"Bring us your fantasies!* Your wildest dreams! Come on, Sarah, we didn't raise you to be that naïve."

"If you'd just give me a chance—"

"To what?" He lowered his paper. "To help people live out their cheap little thrills?"

"Come on. Not every—"

He lifted his paper, covering his face. "This is not a negotiation."

"Why is it even your decision?"

"While you're under my roof, it is."

I dropped the subject. And I didn't tell them as I began meeting with the underground, making connections, practicing. But Mom found my inventory, which included some fairly erotic product. And that was that. I can't remember if it was my decision to leave, or theirs. Maybe an ugly mix.

That was eight years ago. I sometimes miss them terribly, but that bridge is burned. Now it's a card at Christmas. A call from Mom. You know. And the conversion always goes the same:

"Is everything all right with you, Sarah?"

"Yes, Mom, I'm doing great."

"She says she's doing great."

Dad says something in the background.

"Your father wants to know if you're happy with—with everything."

"I'm fine, Mom."

Dad says something else. Mom is silent.

"Did Dad say something?

"No, I don't think so."

"Well, I have to go. I have a client coming."

Pretty much like that. They don't ask me back. I don't ask to come. And we never mention my dreams.

I moved to the city, got a job, an apartment, and worked on my dreaming. I haven't been able to make a decent custom one, like the guy did with Dad and the fish, so I keep on at the diner and sell my ordinaries, the best of them, on the side.

But I can't sell what I don't have. I need a new strategy. Another benefit of our own dreams is they sometimes present solutions. I need one, soon. Here's hoping for tonight.

I walk to the diner, past the alley that runs beneath my fire escape. A colony of black cats stare from around the dumpsters. But these aren't normal cats. They're deformed, bulbous and hairless, like worms with legs. They hang on the walls like lichen and huddle in muculent clumps in the damp shadows. Their mouths open and close as if in a howl, but they make no sound.

I awake and wait for my heart to stop pounding. So much for a solution. Still, as far as quality, it's not bad. I can sell it. I reach for my journal.

But I stop. While dark dreams have a large following, I don't like dealing with those people. They have a vibe, as if they're holding in an awful, secret world. If I give them the slightest encouragement, they'll share it with me, and it might seep into my own dreams, stain them. Those stains are hard to get out.

Besides, when I set down a dream, it's difficult to destroy if I change my mind. Well, I can, of course. It's just pressed on paper. But I feel like I'm throwing away a part of myself.

It's no wonder I had another dark one. Dreams often arise from moods, and these days my few entries are grim. Sales are off; maybe it's just the times, people's changing tastes. Or I'm not as good a dreamer as I once was, or thought I was. God, I hope I'm not losing it.

Last month, I tagged my entire catalog at a discount if bought in bulk. Rent's going up, more than I can afford. A new restaurant opened nearby, and that means fewer customers in the diner, fewer tips. This is my "keep a starving artist off the street" sale. I'm usually not that bold, but if I don't make more sales soon—well, this will at least get me through a couple more months.

After work, I pass the alley outside my building. It looks as it did in my dream, except no cats.

I grab the mail from the slot and bring it up to the apartment. Even the mail has an extra heaviness now. What if there's some unexpected bill? But I won't be able to sleep until I check.

There's a letter from one of my better clients. I used to insist sales be done in person. Giving dreams away involves a certain intimacy, at least for me. Even though I know that's what I've signed up for, I still need to look into their eyes before consummating the transaction. But the financial realities caught up with me, and now I accept mail orders.

This particular client is a real collector. He always selects my best merchandise, the vibrant, soaring dreams and the rare, erotic ones—these last while they're still warm, barely on the market. I smile. This could be the break I need. Hope peeks through the clouds.

The letter reads:

Dear Miss Waters, thank you for your past dreams. Each has a valued place in my collection. I see you are offering up your entire inventory at a reasonable price. I am prepared to acquire your full stock.

I nearly choke. At last, some luck! This alone will keep me in the apartment for a year, with plenty of time to restock. I keep reading.

Please let me know when to expect delivery. P.S. You have marked two of the dreams Not-For-Sale. As part of this deal, I require that you include those as well.

His pen punctures my heart. My joy drains out.

Whenever I need help through the hard times, I revisit my Not-For-Sale dreams. The first is the one I had custom-made, with the fish. I list it in the inventory to show my collaboration skills with another dream worker.

The second I dreamt after leaving home. My mood was awful. The only apartment I could afford was this glorified closet in a run-down tenement that smells like insecticide. I had no friends here, no connections, no customer base. Everything was strange and terrifying. The perfect setup for a nightmare.

But this wasn't a nightmare; it was a salvation. I was back in the old house, a lovely place in the western hills of Connecticut. I woke up in my old bed, on a glorious morning with the sun gilding the leaves outside my window, their shadows freckling the walls and my baseball trophies. Joy washed over me like spring rain. I smelled bacon and coffee, heard the radio playing in the kitchen and my father whooping at a sports score. Mom poked into the doorway in her faded blue apron. "Breakfast is ready, dear."

"Hurry, Sarah, you're missing it!" Dad yelled.

"Coming! Coming!"

I threw off the covers, hopped out of bed, and the dream ended.

It still amazes me how a simple dream, even waking up in your bed with breakfast and family waiting, can bring such joy, such peace. But it did, and it does. I think it's the sudden, unexpected wonder in such a gray world, like tiny flowers in the crumbling sidewalks. And that's why it's in the catalog. To show others what's possible. To give them the hope it gives me.

And now, Mr. Rodman wants it all.

Well, business is business, and negotiation is always possible. Would he be open to a counteroffer, to allow me to hold on to just one of my dreams?

And if so, which? I hold them both in the deepest part of my heart. The breakfast scene has both my mom and dad together. The fishing one only has Dad, but the relationship strikes a special note, now lost. Still, bought dreams such as that wear out quicker, and this one has already become threadbare. Maybe I should let Mr. Rodman take it while it still has some value. But since I created the breakfast one myself, perhaps I could have another like it?

I send him my reply.

Days pass between dark dreams, thick with anxiety. Confusing dreams with shifting landscapes and strange people. Dreams with an atmosphere of dread, or the feeling I forgot something, or some undefinable guilt.

I don't keep any of those.

At last, a response arrives. Turns out I don't need to choose. Mr. Rodman is insistent: all or nothing.

I read the letter a dozen times. What do I do? Take the deal, part of me whispers. Get back on your feet. Pay the damn light bill. I've already come to terms with letting so many of my dreams go at once, though I know that will leave a bitter emptiness. But those two dreams as well? It cuts into me. They're powerful and precious. Perhaps the most precious things I have left. Yet if I decline and blow this chance to get back on my feet, my only option will be to ask my family for financial help.

And there it is—the fear I've avoided since I got here. That I'm a failure. That I should run back to my parents, let any thread of family connection I still cling to snap with the indignity of admitting that I am, in the end, just some seedy dream worker weaving little thrills for people who have given up on their own dreams.

Weaving dreams for people like me.

The letter is damp now in my hand. Selling my dreams is my livelihood, or at least I'm trying to make it that. And if I can use these last ones to make a better life, why shouldn't I? Isn't that what dreams are for?

At last, I decide. I open the journal and start signing away my dreams. I carefully tear them out, page by colorful page, trying to keep my tears from smudging them.

I place the pages into a nice little box along with the bill. As I do, I write a letter to go with it:

Dear Mr. Rodman, I have enclosed my inventory of dreams. I hope you enjoy them. I have attached an invoice and terms.

But I feel I owe you an explanation of the contents. It's a hard thing sometimes to part with one's dreams. And I can tell you it's even harder to watch them all go at once.

So I am sorry, I cannot include those last two. They are my heart. Everything else is negotiable, but without those, there would be no more dreams.

I send him the box and the letter. If he doesn't accept this deal, I might lose my inventory, my apartment, even my job. But now I know what is most important.

The dreams of my heart.

After a full week of agonizing, I receive a call.

"Hello?"

"Miss Waters?"

"Yes?"

"This is Mr. Rodman."

I swallow. We've never talked.

"Mr. Rodman. It's so nice—"

"Did you mean what you said, in your letter, about never selling those other dreams?"

"I'm sorry, but yes."

Something nags at me. It's been a long time, but—

He tries to say something more, but it catches in his throat. The phone shuffles, like he's hanging up.

"Wait!" I say.

A new voice comes on. A woman.

"Sarah?"

"Mom?"

"Oh, Sarah, I'm—listen. Your father—he wants me to ask you to come home."

I begin to cry. Mr. Rodman was Dad all along, saving my dreams. Protecting them.

When I can speak again, I agree, with no hesitation.

Dad and I even talk. Sort of. There are awkward silences, but they're not all empty. There's a light in them, like a happy dream you wake from but can't quite remember. Before we hang up, I ask if he still fishes. He does. We'll do it together while I'm there.

I'll leave tomorrow. And when I'm in my old bed, I'll lay a blank page next to my pillow. Maybe I'll have a nightmare. More likely just something fragmented and stupid.

Or it might be another castle in the sky.

Rick Duffy lives in a peaceful Denver suburb opposite the magnificent Rocky Mountains. Wild rabbits have taken over his backyard. The cats don't care. He's tried anti-bunny spray without success. If you have any ideas (other than perfumed dryer sheets, which a handy neighbor suggested but only funked up the bushes), let Rick know at rickduffy.com. He also likes to write and is the winner of the 2018 RMFW Colorado Gold Writing Contest YA category for his coming-of-age fantasy novel, The Sigil Masters.

GREEN-EYED MONSTER
by Charis Jones

You think I killed my wife because I was jealous? Not at all, officers. First of all—if you'll forgive the correction—the word you want is *envious*, not *jealous*. Envy is the desire for something that belongs to someone else. Jealousy is the fear of losing something that belongs to you. I wasn't jealous of the great Martina Rybek, I was envious of her—and wouldn't you be, if your wife were up for a Nobel Prize in Physics while you were still struggling for tenure? But that isn't why she's lying upstairs waiting for your forensics team to get here. What happened tonight had nothing to do with our lopsided careers at MIT. It—well, it all started with that tennis ball.

Right, the yellow Dunlop that's floating in the bathtub. Yeah, I know it's a strange thing to find... Yes, I realize it wasn't the *only* thing floating in the tub. I'm sure the ball is dead too, and believe me, the poor thing deserves a proper burial. On your walk-through, maybe the two of you noticed the string dangling from the ceiling of our garage? That tennis ball spent nine years at the end of it, just waiting for me to come home every night. It was like a faithful dog that always greets you in the same place. And, except for tonight, I always met my fuzzy buddy in precisely the same spot. Even the nights I drove home a bit hammered. I'd turn the car into the garage smooth as oil, ball hits the red dot on the windshield, bam. Mission accomplished. But when I pulled in tonight, I was dead sober. And dead tired. And damned sick of jumping through hoops.

Did I mention that Martina was something of a control freak? You've seen her name in the news, so you know she was smart…but all that extra neural circuitry comes with a price. Of course, I didn't know that when I met her; I was too blown away by her visions and ideas. Caught up in her brilliance, I could feel the walls of reality getting thinner and more transparent, until it seemed that anything was possible. Now maybe I look like any Joe Schmo standing handcuffed in his kitchen talking to the police, but I've been a neurobiologist for twenty years, and I can tell you that when one part of the brain is overdeveloped, it asphyxiates some other part. In my wife's case, the part that got squeezed was her ability to let the world turn on its own. From the day I met her, she was the twitchiest person I ever saw—always wanting to fix, change, or control something. I didn't realize how deep her compulsions ran until we'd been married about a week and I found Martina on a stepladder, hanging that tennis ball from the ceiling of our garage. Why? Because I wasn't parking the car in quite the right place.

"Sometimes it's too far to the left," she explained, "and I can't get to the recycling bin. And sometimes it's too far forward and I have to go around the back of the car just to get in the house."

I gave her a look that said, *You can't be serious,* but Martina only shrugged as she uncapped a tube of paint.

"I know it looks a little weird," she admitted, "but it'll make things so much easier."

"All right, honey," I said, because I'm a pretty easygoing guy. Not the sort who wants to start fighting just a few days after tying the knot. So I let my bride paint a red dot on the windshield of my old Honda, thinking I was a good man for humoring her.

But, as they say, no good deed goes unpunished. That tennis ball was just the first pebble in an avalanche of household rules—rules I came to realize had only one explanation. Simply put, Martina had to have things a certain way or she came unglued. If the car wasn't parked right, if the milk was sitting where the OJ should be, if the trash in the bins hadn't been pushed down as far as it would go, if the tea bags were not standing at attention like soldiers at drill, she couldn't concentrate. And she didn't trust me to get any of this right. Have you taken note of the labels and instructions on every bin, drawer, and cabinet in this house? Notice how the salt goes in three different places, depending on type and size? And God help you if you put the fancy pink or green or black lava salts in the cabinet with the dry goods! One sound that will haunt me forever is the patter of her heels as she canvassed the house, checking and reorganizing, straightening edges that were already straight, and wiping up invisible dust.

You're probably wondering how on Earth she managed a successful research lab. Well, the same way she managed her home. Geniuses are supposed to be eccentric, and it seems like the weirdest ones have the most illustrious careers. Maybe that's my problem—the lobes of my brain are the right size and all the neurons are firing quietly without getting in each other's way. Maybe I'm just too plain-vanilla normal to sail my ship to the stars.

What's that? Right. Stick to the story. Well, I was tired when I got home from work, okay? Theoretical physicists like my wife can play in the cosmic ether without leaving the house, but there's nothing theoretical about biology. Wet labs are messy, demanding places. Cells and explanted tissues require constant feeding, and so do cages of rats. Unlike my wife, I can't afford to hire an army of minions to carry out my grand plans. My technician and I do all the work ourselves. Seven days a week, gentlemen.

So, when I wheeled into the garage tonight and the Dunlop hit the windshield two inches left of the red target, I was surprised and a little annoyed. I backed out and tried again. This time the wretched ball landed three inches to the right. That's what's called *overcompensation,* in case you officers were wondering. Probably you know all about it, with those big guns you're packing. Well, third time's the charm, right? Only this time, it wasn't. On my third try, the ball came to rest maybe a centimeter and a half away from the red dot. Now, I can hear what you're thinking. *A centimeter and a half? Who cares? Close enough for government work.* But that's where you're wrong. *Martina* cared. *Martina* would check—she always did, as soon as I walked in the door. She wouldn't yell or throw a fit, no. She would make this agitated noise somewhere between a groan and a sigh, and her eyes would scrunch shut as if she suddenly had a migraine. And she'd say something like, *George, please, the car's not in the right spot. Would you mind parking it again? It's not too much to ask, is it?*

I gave my parking job one more try, only to miss by a finger's width yet again. Then I killed the engine and got out. I slammed the door so hard the Dunlop bounced. On the other side of the garage, my wife's gray Lexus sat smug and aloof, its unmarked windshield gleaming. Wherever she was in the house, I knew Martina would have heard my car door slam. I could already see her wincing, fingertips kneading at that place above her right ear where all the neurons were misfiring.

I have to float the boat for both of us, whispered the Martina in my mind. She often spoke to me this way in my darker moments. *Since your start-up funds ran out, my endowment is the only thing keeping your pathetic career alive. I pay for all of your rat colonies, your enzymes and petri dishes and ballpoint pens. I pull strings for you. You don't need tenure; I am your tenure. And what do I ask in return? That you keep the house neat. Put things back where they belong. Park the car in the right goddamn spot!*

It was a mistake to imagine her saying these things. A red fog clouded my vision, turning the garage into a darkening world where a faded yellow sun hung low in the sky. I reached out and squeezed that sun. The feel of it, tired and pancake-flat after almost a decade of lighting my way home, sparked my empathy. Here was something that had come off the factory line fresh and ready for life at 100 mph, and instead it had been suspended in a gloomy garage to molder away. Suddenly all the seconds and minutes and hours—hell, years—I'd spent catering to Martina's demands rushed in to fill every nook and cranny in my brain. The combined weight of all that dead time made me stagger.

My life was a sham. I loved my work, and God knows I worked my ass off, but I didn't have the funding to survive on my own. I labored within the cage of my wife's success. I had to ask her—*Ask her!*—for every single thing I needed. She owned me, and I hated her for that. But I hated myself more for staying in the cage.

Standing there in the garage, I imagined Martina sighing and saying, *Is it too much to ask?*

"Yes," I told the tennis ball. "I think it is." Before I could talk myself out of it, I gave the ball a sharp tug and felt it come loose as the old string gave way. I stared at the emancipated orb in a daze. I imagined cramming it down my wife's throat and whispering in her ear, *It took four thousand tries, but I finally hit the right spot.* With a mad laugh, I slipped the ball into my pocket. Then I went inside, closing the door as gently as a thief.

The house was dark. No light spilled down the stairs, as it did when Martina was working in her office. She always kept the door ajar so her antennae could sample the air for signs of disorder. But her car was in the garage, so she had to be home. Maybe she had gone to bed early. Maybe she was sick.

Only…my wife never went to bed before 1:00 a.m. And she had never, in all our years together, suffered from the slightest illness. Some of her circuits might be jammed, but she was apparently immune to human pathogens. So, where the hell *was* she?

I flicked on the light in the entryway and headed into the kitchen—and even in the semi-dark, I could see that something was terribly amiss. The mail on the counter lay in an *ordinary pile,* as if a normal person had brought it in.

"It's a wonder the earth is still spinning," I muttered, straightening the mail by force of habit before remembering that I'd already committed high treason. The ball, after all, was no longer attached to its string. I had torn the sentinel down from its high place and *put it in my pocket.* Tomorrow would be time enough to repent and crawl back into my shell, but tonight, by God, I was going to revel in an orgy of vandalism.

First, I arranged the stack of mail so the big flyers were on top and the smallest envelopes were on the bottom. Then I pulled some gobs of plastic packaging up from the trash bin and let them dangle artistically over the edge, like transparent flowers in bloom. I moved the soap dispenser three inches to the left. I knocked down the column of tea packets—*At ease, soldiers*—and laid one of them face-down, as if he'd been shot in the back by a sniper. Opening the fridge, I moved the butter from its proper compartment to—wait for it—the produce drawer! I shivered at the delicious blasphemy of it. Seeing the butter dish canted at a drunken angle on top of a head of lettuce made me realize what a dry evening it had been. So, I poured myself a double scotch and violated three home ordinances by leaving my dirty glass at the edge of the table *sans* coaster. Then I went through the house in search of my wife, turning on every light along the way.

The first floor was deserted. Martina's upstairs office was just as empty, her computer screens dark, her desk covered with manuscripts and journals in pristine piles. Her white noise machine, which migrated between her office and the bedroom, was absent from its daytime place of honor. If the tennis ball and I were fellow inmates, that noise machine was more like a spoiled pet. The little demon was the size of a jewelry box and as black as the vacuum between the stars. It said whatever Martina wanted to hear, but in a voice like rain falling, or distant monkeys howling, or waves pounding some digital shore. It canceled out the noise of real life so she could work or sleep, and most nights, the soft racket drove me to the sofa downstairs.

Peering into the bedroom, I saw no sign of my wife or the noise machine. Then I noticed a faint, flickery glow under our bathroom door. Emboldened by the whiskey, I crossed the room and turned the doorknob.

The door opened silently, of course; nothing in our house ever dared to creak.

"Honey—" I began, and then whatever brash declaration I was about to make slid back down my throat, forgotten.

Martina lay in the claw-foot bathtub, which until that point had been purely decorative. All I could see was the hardwood sheen of her hair, which had fallen across her face. Candlelight from an old stub of wax played over the gleaming porcelain. By the side of the tub sat a remote control, a bottle of merlot, and a half-empty glass. Dry thunder from the noise machine echoed through the room. Martina looked up at the sound of my voice, and I was struck by how beautiful she was. Inhumanly beautiful, like something machine-crafted. You could see the fine shape of the bones under her skin. Her hazel eyes shone bright green in the candlelight.

She muttered something I couldn't make out over the rumble of thunder.

"What?" I said, moving slowly into air that was thick with the scent of jasmine. I still couldn't believe what I was seeing. Martina rarely drank, and she *never* lounged in bathtubs by candlelight.

"It didn't get renewed," she said, reaching down to fumble with the remote and send the programmed storm packing.

"What didn't get renewed?" I asked.

She gave me her patented impatient look, but there was a thread of something else beneath it. Was it fear? Uncertainty? It was like a breath of wind blowing through a familiar landscape, turning it briefly into unknown territory.

"My endowment, George," she said.

For a moment I basked in the miraculous, unbelievable knowledge that the exalted Dr. Martina Rybek had been *rejected*. Her infallible force had somehow stopped short! Then I realized what she was talking about—her endowment from MIT. The money that was keeping me in business.

The news should have been a terrible blow, but I only felt a kind of numb relief. Martina shifted in her shroud of bubbles and the smell of night-blooming flowers intensified, adding to the impression that I was in a bizarre dream.

"I don't understand it," she mumbled, reaching for her wineglass. "I hired five new people last year...published twenty-two papers...gave three keynote talks. I let them prance me around every time there's some promotion for women in science. A show pony that can do physics! Let's see them fit old Dr. Abrams into a dress and have him make flirty small talk with the fat-cat donors. I go to their idiotic social functions—even showed my face at Melman's holiday party. I bring in over a million dollars a year for them. What the hell do they *want*?"

"Maybe they figure you already have more than you need," I suggested mildly. "Or maybe they figured out what you're doing with a good chunk of that endowment."

The look she turned on me was full of frustrated contempt. "They knew I was siphoning money to you for years. Besides, the funds in that endowment are untagged—I can do whatever I want with them!" She gestured angrily with her glass, sloshing red wine onto the tiles. I gaped at the impossible mess as silence stretched out like the path to a strange new world.

"So, who are they giving the endowment to?" I asked at last.

"They won't say," she replied. "But you know they're using it to woo someone who already has a Nobel Prize. Just what we need, another fossil whose best years were half a century ago." Martina paused to take a long swallow of wine. "They know I'm not going anywhere...not with *you* in tow. They've got me by the balls, and they know it." She put the glass down and stared at the wall. The expression on her face was so unfamiliar, it was like looking at another woman. She appeared utterly lost. This might have been the first time she had ever failed at something.

"Well, our employment opportunities have just opened up," I said brightly. "Since I'll be putting in applications for Wendy's and Burger King, which are everywhere."

Martina turned her bewildered gaze on me. I don't think it had occurred to her yet that this event marked the end of my career. All this tub-languishing and wine-swilling was because a piece of her world had slipped out of her grasp. Note, gentlemen: the biggest piece of *my* world was the very smallest piece of hers.

It took a few seconds, but eventually my point-of-view sank in and she rolled her eyes.

"Oh, for God's sake," she snorted, flicking at a presumptuous bubble on her arm. "You could try submitting a grant application before you decide to lie down and die. Some of us do it all the time."

I moved a few steps closer to the tub, to where that puddle of merlot gleamed darkly on the floor. It looked like an old sun—a blood-red sun on the brink of supernova. I reached into my pocket and gave the tennis ball a squeeze.

"I had an NIH grant, Martina." Speaking was suddenly difficult, as if I were forcing words through someone else's mouth. "You know that, and you know it wasn't renewed. I guess now you have an idea what that feels like."

She gave me a disgusted look. "You need to learn to play the game, champ. Would it kill you to get to know your program officer?"

"Schmoozing with your PO over cocktails might work at NSF," I said acidly, "but you know NIH sticks to grant scores."

"Are you suggesting that I *schmoozed* my way to the top?" She barked a short laugh. "You biologists are all the same—*poor me, everyone is out to get me, no one understands how important my little experiments are!* If any of you worked as hard as you whine."

"I'm not whining," I said through my teeth, fingers clenched around the tennis ball. I forcibly unclenched them, then collared the bottle of merlot by its scruffy neck and took a swig. The wine tasted like every bitter thought I'd ever jammed into the back of my skull. "I'm just telling you how it is. That money from your endowment kept me going, and I'm grateful. But without it, I have to close up shop."

"It's too bad you're not a physicist," she said, eyeing me speculatively. "Still, you could always come work for me." She said this as if it were the world's most generous offer—as if I would be an ungrateful ass to refuse it. "Jeannie's getting ready to retire, and I'll need a new assistant. You're not as organized as she is, but you know how to push paper and cut through red tape, all the administrative stuff." She took another nip of merlot and raised her eyebrows at me. As much as I hated her, I had to laugh—I couldn't help myself. Her condescension was just so predictable.

"Thanks, honey," I said, leaning over to top off her glass, "but at the end of the day, I think stuffing fries into little paper sacks would be more rewarding."

"Don't be ridiculous," she scoffed. "You're not doing any such thing."

"No?" I said, still wearing what felt like a Death's Head grin. "Why the hell not?"

"Because you're my husband," she said, "and my husband is a *scientist*."

"You just offered me a job as your secretary," I pointed out.

"You would still have the title," she snapped. "Research Associate Professor, Senior Scientist, whatever. Something respectable." She hiccupped, and the hand holding her glass shook. More wine spattered the floor in a trail of bloody drops.

"Martina," I said quietly, pointing to the tiles. She followed my finger and her eyes widened in horror. But when she set the glass down and tried to get up, I put a hand on her shoulder. I wasn't done messing with her yet. A latent perversity had woken up inside me, and it said the evening wasn't over. Not by a long shot.

"Tell you what," I said. "If you can stay in this bath for another ten minutes—just ten minutes—I'll schedule your appointments and bring your coffee. I'll do it with a smile. I'll even wear a skirt."

"What the hell are you talking about?" she hissed, still scrabbling to get out of the tub. I almost let her do it—the sight of my inebriated wife cleaning the bathroom floor in the buff was one I had never seen before and would surely never see again—but I had to stay focused. So, I picked up her wineglass and perched on the edge of the tub to block her escape.

"What's the rush?" I said, waving the glass in her face just to show her what a loose cannon I was. "That wine's not going anywhere."

"It'll stain the tiles, you idiot!"

"You painted a spot that color on my windshield," I reminded her, "the first week we were married. Remember?"

She wasn't listening. Her eyes darted around, looking for a way out, but I was leaning over the tub with her glass of merlot, and she didn't dare push me away.

"Was it really necessary to deface my car?" I went on. "You could have just used a sticker."

"What is with you tonight?" she muttered, then seemed to notice that a cloud of whiskey fumes had overpowered the scent of her bath oil. "Are you drunk?"

"Well, if it isn't the pot talking," I said, sipping her wine and belching for good measure.

Something dark flickered in the depths of her eyes. Tipsy or not, she was recalculating, deciding on a different approach. Suddenly she arched her back so the foam slid off her perfect breasts, then eased down until the sudsy water reached her chin. Her eyes softened into pools of liquid jade.

"I know this is hard," she murmured, reaching up to stroke my neck with one wet finger, "but we'll find a way to get you funded. I'll figure something out."

"There's nothing to figure out," I said hoarsely. "I'm done. Out of the game."

Her hand wandered down my arm, then crept south of my belt, caressing as she hadn't done in years. I stared into the lagoon of her eyes, hypnotized. Snicker all you want, gentlemen, but every man is a prisoner to his own lust. When that need goes unsatisfied—say, for months on end—he's even more of a fool. I had to catch myself before I put the wine down and surrendered my upper hand.

"You're not done," she said, squeezing a groan out of me. I leaned forward to kiss her, but just before our lips met, her gaze darted downward. Toward the spilled wine. And when she looked up again…

How can I describe this so you'll understand? Somehow, the curtains of her eyes lifted and I saw *through* them. Not to her soul. What I saw inside was a rat. An insane rat in a lab cage, chittering madly. At that moment, it was busy counting up the minutes, calculating how much time was left before the damage to the tiles was permanent. As brilliant and independent as she was, Martina was a slave to that creature. She would do anything to appease it.

I stared at the rat and it stared back at me, through my wife's green eyes. I shriveled and went cold all over, and my brain—fogged with drink and desire and frustration—finally cleared.

"You're worried about a little spilled wine?" I said, lurching to my feet. My voice was as shaky as my knees, but I spoke clearly to the rat. "That's nothing. Just wait'll you see the party going on downstairs. It's a holiday for *everyone* in the Rybek compound—I even gave the tennis ball the night off." I pulled that newly freed minion from my pocket and tossed it into the tub. Martina froze, staring at the floating Dunlop as if it were a snake.

Put it back.

The words were soundless, an order issued directly into my mind. Still, I knew exactly who—or what—was speaking. I could see it loping back and forth, back and forth, in the dark cage behind my wife's eyes.

Not a chance, I replied in my head.

Put it back. Mop up the wine. Clean up the mess downstairs. Do it now!

Not a chance in hell, I clarified. My long-held resentment toward Martina suddenly shifted its focus. I remembered that even with all her baggage, the old Martina was someone I'd fallen in love with. In the early years of our relationship, we were comrades and good companions. But the prickly sweetness of her personality eroded over time, leaving her cynical and contemptuous of everyone. And this creature giving me orders from behind her eyes…this creature was responsible. *As soon as I sober up, I'm going to find a way to get rid of you!*

A chuckle sounded in the depths of my head.

That might have been possible twenty years ago, said the rat, *with drugs or electroshock therapy or a really good psychiatrist. But it's much too late now. I've taken over in here.*

I looked deeper into the rat's cage and saw that what appeared to be bars were not bars at all. They were a meshwork of nerves trailing bright, pulsing axons. Some were frayed and some were dark and severed, as if they'd been bitten clean through. Black eyes gleamed from a jungle of synapses.

How did you get in there? I demanded. *Where did you come from?*

I was born here, the rat answered. *Of course, I was much smaller then—hardly more than an urge or two— but she made a little nest for me and fed me scraps until I was big enough to fend for myself.*

Fend for yourself? I said with dawning horror. I could only think of the rat's teeth, the rat's claws. *Are you trying to kill her?*

Of course not, said the rat. *I know which connections are essential, and which are expendable. Her scientific acumen will remain intact. Other things, like her affections, which were always weak at best, have made for many a good meal.* The creature nosed between the hanging vines of two thick axons, sniffing and questing. Following one up to its source, it took hold of the plump cell and licked its chops.

But won't you starve when you run out of...disposable neurons? I asked.

The rat grinned at me. *You're a neurobiologist, aren't you, George? You know that neural pathways don't replace themselves quickly, but they do grow back. In the meantime, there's plenty to snack on.* As if to illustrate this point, the rat munched delicately at a fringe of dendrites along the cell's surface. Martina shivered, and all the lines of tension on her face disappeared for a moment. Suddenly I saw a trace of the little girl she must have been—as bright and impatient and headstrong as ever, but *free.* Free of this thing that had turned her mind into its meal.

So far, you've done your part to keep things in order, said the rat as it toyed with the denuded cell, batting it lightly from one paw to the other. *Is that going to change? Are you going to clean up the mess you made? Because I have all the tools of persuasion right here.* It bared ancient teeth at me, then dropped the neuron and scampered through the thicket of my wife's brain, toward regions that were still glowing and untouched. *A mind is like a buffet, George. I can stop nibbling on her desire center and she might want to have sex more than three times a year. Or I can start feeding on her sanity, or her sense of human decency. I can make things better for you, or I can make them much, much worse.*

As the rat tore through a web of luminous neurons, I felt something for Martina that I'd never felt before. Pity. Sick with it, I looked away and her noise machine caught my eye. It was sitting on the low shelf above the tub, plugged into an outlet so close that its long cord was bunched up behind it. I turned it on and thunder rent the air, cutting through steam and the stench of alcohol. The power button under my hand was as warm as a running engine. There seemed to be a deadly energy coiled inside that little black box.

I felt a pair of eyes boring a hole in the back of my head. Beady eyes, dark and feral and unblinking. The skies above our house cracked and boomed, and ozone electrified the air, turning the spit in my throat metallic. A recorded thunderstorm never felt or sounded so real.

CLEAN UP THE MESS, shrilled the voice in my head. *CLEAN IT UP, CLEAN IT UP, CLEAN IT UP!*

I swallowed hard, fighting the imperative to obey. The part of me that had always bowed to Martina was trying to drag me toward the tennis ball and the spilled wine, toward fresh string and the scourge of bleach. It was like the thirst for a drink at the end of a long day, like the crippling need for a woman who is only using you as a puppet. But in the steamy mirror, I saw the face of another puppet behind me—my wife enslaved and trapped in the prison of her own mind. I put the wine down and gazed at the source of the storm, that throbbing box under my hand. There was an answer there, if I could only see it.

In the lab, there are times when your mind's vision is true and your hands are golden—the brain and its tools in perfect sync. As the thunder rolled, I felt that power coursing through my fingers, working its way up to my brain. And all at once, I knew how to set her free. I just had to do one last experiment with a rat.

Sliding the noise machine toward me, I rotated it so the left corner overhung the shelf. Martina's favorite device was now precarious, misaligned, an offense to the eye...in flagrant violation of the one true law that governed this house. You can never be sure how an experiment will turn out, but that feeling of inevitability was so strong. The alcohol she had consumed, the moisture slicking the shelf, and the box itself were all colluding with me to bias the outcome. As I turned and walked away, I knew exactly what would happen in the next few seconds. And I may not be a physicist, gentlemen, but I know what a ground-fault circuit interrupter is—and I know this old house doesn't have one.

Behind me, I heard the swish of water in the tub, then the squeal of a startled rodent. I turned just as the noise machine struck the bath, hissing like oil on a hot griddle. Martina shrieked and jerked like a marionette, stirring up a maelstrom. Her face contorted, and there was nothing human in her eyes. They seethed with the frenzy of a doomed creature, clawing and gnawing in vain. Smoke rose from the bathwater as the noise machine sank beneath the waves. The wineglass had overturned on the shelf, and a Red Sea flooded the bathroom floor, but my wife no longer cared about such trivialities. I had baited a trap for her master, and the rat—well, the rat had choked on the cheese.

You're looking a little pale, gentlemen. Would you care for some refreshment? I'm sorry to say I finished off the whiskey before you got here—and we're all out of wine—but there might be an old bottle of pineapple rum in the cupboard. No?

Well, I guess that's the end of the story, then. By the time I see a lawyer I'll probably wish I'd kept quiet, but right now I just want you to understand. Tonight, for the first time, I didn't envy Martina. I finally saw her as she was, the most helpless prisoner in the Rybek house. But I managed to free both of us. Even standing here in handcuffs, I feel liberated.

Would you believe that I feel empty, too, because I've sacrificed everything I hold dear? Everything I fell in love with…true genius, unshakable confidence and willpower, the ability to blaze a path through all of life's obstacles. Even when thorns grew thick around those virtues, I still clung to them. I hoarded them for nine miserable years, because they were things I couldn't bear to lose.

So, I guess maybe you were right. Maybe I was jealous of Martina, after all.

Charis Himeda (Jones), PhD is a Research Associate Professor at the University of Nevada, Reno School of Medicine. Her research, employing CRISPR gene editing technology as a potential therapy for muscle disease, has earned her interviews with The Washington Post, The Huffington Post, *and* The Boston Business Journal.

Dr. Himeda studies mechanisms of muscle disease by day and doffs her lab gloves to pen speculative fiction by night. She loves writing about quirky, conflicted, renegade scientists driven by their deep desire to explore and shape the world around them. She is a two-time winner in the PNWA literary contest, a winner in the Sandy contest, the Zebulon contest, and the Colorado Gold contest, a shortlister in the 2019 Cygnus Awards, and a quarterfinalist in the 2014 Amazon Breakthrough Novel Award Contest. Her short stories have appeared in Antimuse, Eureka Literary Magazine, The Marlboro Review, MudRock: Stories and Tales, *and* Nth Degree.

REMEDIATION

by B.J. Eardley

The train has been stopped for over an hour. The conductor finally announces we can step outside. No wandering. Stay next to the train. Normally Alicia would stretch that command, test the boundary of this new form of detention, but she hasn't slept since we left San Diego two days ago. Her eyes are rimmed dark, and her red curls are snarled in front of her face. She is tired and anxious, desperately looking for a sign of what to do next.

A job waits in Denver, along with a room in an apartment and a counselor, but I know Alicia well enough to understand she has no intention of taking that job, living in that apartment, talking to that counselor. It was the social worker's idea for Alicia to ride the train instead of taking a plane. A chance for her to reflect, ease back into the world now that she is eighteen and juvenile detention is behind her. The social worker paid for the ticket out of her own pocket. I've observed this with humans. The way they exchange money to relieve their guilt.

From where we stand outside the train, we look out at a rolling desert, with soil cracked like a face abused by too much sun. A veil of translucent color floats above that cracked soil— spring flowers in the desert. Sego lilies on one side, a swath of yellow asters on the other, globemallow in the gully between. Patience is their message. The flowers are full of joy, and so they sing. I imagine the song coming from the lilies' cupped blossoms, the asters' whirl of petals, and the mallows' orange blooms. Alicia can't yet hear the music, so neither can I. Still, I know they are singing because I once lived among the flowers.

"It'll be at least another hour," the train attendant tells us. She wipes away the sweat on her brow with the back of her hand. Her white-and-blue collared uniform buttons tightly at her neck. It's not designed for the heat of a desert sun. "Somebody up ahead tried to race the train," she continues. "Can't go on until they've evaluated the circumstance, cleaned up the wreckage. Happens." She wipes her brow again.

"I wonder if it was on purpose," Alicia says. She flicks her red curls behind her ears, but they spring rebelliously back along her cheeks. "I mean, it would be an interesting way to go, 'didn't know what hit her' kind of thing." She smiles at the attendant. Flicks her hair. Lifts her chin. "And I bet the insurance policy would still pay."

After six generations of human hosts, I can read the expression in the attendant's eyes that says she is uncomfortable with this switch to suicide talk. She is saved a response by the rattling call of a sandhill crane over our heads.

The sky is a cloudless desert blue. A blue I haven't seen in a long time.

"There are the cranes," Alicia says, pointing to two barely discernable specks in the sky. "You can hear the call of a sandhill from over two miles away." She's wondering how far away her call might be heard if she found herself needing to cry for help. Now that she's eighteen, Alicia is beginning to feel my presence. It makes her uneasy. Anxious. She shakes off the feeling with sips from her water bottle, which is filled with vodka. I wasn't surprised when she stole the vodka from the store across from the train station. I knew it wouldn't be long before she started drinking again.

Alicia reaches into her worn pink backpack for her binoculars, the ones she left on the seat of the bus we took to the train station. I knew she forgot them at the time, but there was nothing I could do because I didn't yet have the ability to influence her. She digs in her backpack, feeling the rough canvas bag the social worker gave her with toothpaste, soap, deodorant, and lotion. She runs her hand over the smooth cotton of her T-shirts and the rough edge of the zipper on her other pair of jeans. A cami is wrapped around a bag that contains another bra, underwear, and what's left of the $100 that was her stipend until she got to Denver. No binoculars. She looks nervously back at the train, hoping she left the binoculars in her seat. Then she squints to see the cranes.

She wonders what they are doing here in a place with no sign of water.

When the sun dipped behind the cliff, it cast a long shadow over the wheat field where a pair of cranes were dancing. It was 1971. Alicia's grandmother, Doris, had just learned she was pregnant, a surprise at thirty-five. She and I were delighting in the dance of the cranes as they ran at each other with their wings extended, bobbed their heads, and threw grass in arcs above them. Doris loved the cranes because they mate for life. She thought maybe she and her husband, Charlie, could have stayed together if he had only learned to dance.

Doris's Day of Remediation came two weeks after her daughter, Tina, was born. It was the London Flu.

When we get back on the train, Alicia looks for her binoculars. Under the seats, both forward and back, then up in the bin above our head where the thin green tag identifies our destination as Denver. She curses to herself and bites at the skin on the corner of her thumb. Realizing the binoculars are gone, Alicia imagines that someone took them out of her backpack. She looks up and down the car, as if she can identify the thief among the rumpled and disheveled passengers.

Seeing no likely candidates, Alicia takes out her bird handbook. She thinks birds are advisors, a notion acquired from a book her foster mother read to her when she was eight. Alicia uses her bird handbook as a type of seer stone. So human. In the face of uncertain situations, humans find security in seers and fortune-telling.

When Alicia looks up sandhill cranes, she confirms they are wetland birds and their migration over this area should have happened much earlier. A fact she finds significant.

"The maximum known lifespan for a sandhill crane is eighteen years," Alicia whispers to herself as she reads. "Eighteen." She smiles. Since she has just turned eighteen, she's convinced the number is important, that the cranes had a message, and that message is the number eighteen. That's how she thinks. This dependence on messages from birds has been worse since we left detention. Makes sense. More uncertainty.

Alicia pulls out the map of Utah with the yellow marker line extending diagonally across it to show the train route. Alicia loves maps. She imagines that, with a map, she will always know where she is. Ironic for someone who has been lost for most of her life. She uses the distance key and her thumb to measure out eighteen miles and delights in the fact that the next train station is about eighteen miles away. She nods her head confidently as if this coincidence reassures her. The cranes' message is clear. She folds the map and tucks it into her backpack.

"I'm getting off at the next stop," Alicia says to the passing attendant.

The attendant glances at the green slip of paper above our seat.

"But you're ticketed to Denver. You won't be able to get your luggage."

Alicia smiles, flips her hair. "Change of plans." She doesn't tell the attendant that there is no other luggage. Just her backpack, with a change of clothes and the remainder of her stipend money.

The attendant looks as if she's about to ask a question, but Alicia pulls at her hair again and gives that smile, the one that can be both innocent and intimidating. The attendant shrugs, folds over the seat tag, and continues down the aisle.

We're heading down the stairs when the conductor announces the next station, a town named after the muddy river that appears suddenly out the window. We get off, and the train slinks on.

The town hardly seems to warrant a train stop. The street from the station is wide and unpaved. A veil of dust clings to the blistered paint on the buildings decaying along the street. The view is like something out of a Western movie set. Invasive brome cheatgrass grows through the cracks in the uneven sidewalk. Brome was brought to America against its will in contaminated grain and straw. It has shown its resilience by displacing much of the native grasses. The brome's own form of remediation, I suppose—though the indigenous grasses might not see it that way.

We pass two bars, boarded up. The third has a red "Open" sign propped on the windowsill. Inside, a black-haired man in an apron and faded green ball cap flips burgers on a large grill. A couple wearing denim and dust exit the bar through two wide swinging doors. The smell of sizzling meat and grease wraps around us.

The couple pulls away in a rusty yellow truck and a plume of dust. Alicia coughs, takes a sip out of her water bottle. She's drawn to the bar, thinks about going in, hesitates, then heads past the bar to an intersection with a wide paved road stretching east and west. A boarded-up gas station is on the corner across the street. A slanting metal roof sags over the hunched shoulders of the pumps, where a faded red sign shows gasoline at thirty-five cents a gallon. Alicia can't imagine that gasoline was ever that inexpensive.

"This was the old highway before the interstate bypass in the early '70s." The voice is behind us, male.

Alicia turns around, flips her snake of red curls, and smiles confidently.

It's the man from the bar, his ball cap pushed back. Asian. Japanese, maybe. Thirties. Thin, but muscled. The spatula he used at the grill is still in his hand.

"Half the town eventually shut down." He points the spatula toward a two-story stone building on the opposite corner. "Used to be a bank."

The bank's square tower holds a clock that is missing the hour hand. Fine cuts of stone curve over the tall, thin windows. The plywood that covers the windows is gray and deteriorating. Brome grass fringes the foundation of the building. The eastern wall is lined with hollyhocks, not yet in blossom. Mid to late summer is their time. The hollyhocks are exemplary survivors. Unlike the brome, they came willingly to the Americas, just as they went to

Europe from China so long ago. Endurance. That's the message of hollyhocks.

"I'm Sam," the man says. He has soft eyes.

Alicia doesn't stop to question why this man, Sam, left his grill to come after us. I question it immediately, but she doesn't sense my concern.

"I'm Alicia. Know of any work?" She speaks in a light way, as if the answer isn't necessarily of any importance. A 'You staying cool in the heat?' kind of question. She gestures to the bar. "I could wait tables. I have experience."

Humans would call Alicia resilient, much like the hollyhocks. People would see her resilience in her calm face, the upward tilt of her head to show confidence. Those people don't know what I know about Alicia. Humans are often wrong in how they judge other humans.

Sam is judging Alicia now. "You can find work at the hotel next to the truck stop up the road," he finally says. "Always looking for maids."

Which means it's a lousy place to work. We know this much.

To our right, the old highway extends past the skeletons of buildings, the broken faces of the town's previous life. To the left is a convenience store, a T-shirt shop, and, several blocks beyond that, the towering lights of a truck stop. Behind it, a two-story hotel.

"They'll advance your pay. Give you a bonus if you stay a month. General delivery is all they'll need for an address. Just a month."

Something about the way he says it. Just a month.

There is a commotion in a large cottonwood tree behind the bar. A magpie flaps out of the leaves in pursuit of a raven. Alicia gets a twisting feeling in her stomach, as if she is the object of the magpie's pursuit. She lifts her water bottle to take a drink but changes her mind. She decides to stop drinking, pour out what's left of the vodka. Make a new start that's of her own choice.

She thinks she can do this on her own.

It was a windy day in 1918. Margaret, Alicia's great-great-grandmother, had befriended one of the magpies that ate from the bins behind the hotel. Margaret read that magpies could be taught to talk, just like parrots, but she thought magpies communicated just fine without tangling their tongues around the unpredictability of human speech. One of the magpies, the one Margaret called Sister, swooped low across the ground, avoiding the force of the wind currents. Margaret smiled and clicked her tongue. The magpie clicked back. Margaret held out her arm and Sister perched there, cocking her head.

Margaret's hands were red from scrubbing floors. She hadn't had a day off in two months, but she wasn't drinking. The telegram with news of her husband's death was collecting dust on her dresser. Her daughter, Lillian, lived with an aunt a four-hour drive away.

Margaret closed her eyes and lifted her head to the sun, as if the rays of light could nourish her. She detected the shadows of tree limbs on her face. The branches were speckled with swollen buds of promise.

Margaret was brave on her Day of Remediation. It was the Spanish Flu. There was a war on. Soldiers carried our gift abroad and back home again. There was no vaccine.

Alicia listens to a tinkle of bells from the shade porch behind the bar. She stretches her fingers as if she can touch the sound waves, imagining she can feel a storm approaching in the wind's early breath. This level of sensitivity is a surprise, an indication that her Day of Remediation is near. I didn't expect this so early. But I am ready. This time our gift is not a copy of one of the masters'. The gift is my creation, crafted with Alicia's help.

"Is there a restroom I could use?" Alicia asks Sam. Restrooms are places of solace for Alicia. Places where she can be protected by a lock on a door.

"Out back. I'll show you," Sam says, pointing to the shade porch.

That's how we come upon the photographs, lined up along the dark hallway at the back of the bar. Alicia stops at the first one, which shows two small children carrying a chest covered with stamped metal.

"My great-grandfather's family," Sam says. "His brother was four. His sister was six." Tags hang from the buttons of the children's coats and the handles of the chest. "Each person was assigned a number. Baggage to be moved. They were sent here from their homes in California. *Internment camps* is the word they used." Sam talks as if he is giving a lecture on recent history, but I hear what is unsaid. The bitterness. The resentment. The anger resulting from hypocrisy and prejudice.

I often don't recognize other hosts, and never have I been successful at communicating with others of my kind. But there is something here with Sam. And now it makes sense why he followed us.

Sam points to a picture of a man and woman carrying two suitcases each.

"My great-great-grandparents. They were allowed twenty-five pounds per person. They had a general store. One week to leave. Sold what they could. Put the rest in storage the government offered. Never saw any of those things again. Eleven thousand Japanese surrounded by barbed wire fence in a 640-acre camp. For their own protection, the government said. But the guards in the towers? Their guns were pointed in, not out."

The story is familiar. The injustices that humans are prone to creating exemplify the need for remediation. As with Alicia's relatives, the victims of the Japanese internment would be perfect hosts. Anger and resentment from such persecution can be captured in the gift we create and then used to fuel understanding of the need for remediation. While choosing humans as my hosts may have been more complicated than using other animals, such as birds or mosquitoes, I believe it's this ability to tap into human emotions that strengthens my gift.

"The camp is still out there," Sam says. "Bits and pieces. It's not far from the campground on the river. You need a place? The campground's a bit of a walk, but it's a good spot." He looks at Alicia's backpack and the blanket she stole from the train slung across her shoulder. "I have an extra tent you could use."

We take the tent. The walk isn't far. When we arrive, we are serenaded by robins fluttering from cottonwood to cottonwood.

A robin was singing in a potato field in Ireland on a windy day in March 1847. The potato famine was well underway, and Alicia's great-great-great-great-grandmother cried at the beauty of the song. This was Cassidy, my first host. Her parents named her Cassidy because of her curly red hair, a trait that each of my subsequent hosts inherited, just as they inherited my presence. Typhus took Cassidy's parents and two little sisters because their starved bodies had nothing left with which to fight. The fire of hatred burned inside Cassidy. Hatred for the British, who refused help while Ireland continued to export the grain that could have saved her family from starvation, hatred for the landowner who kicked them off their land, hatred for the workhouses that fed them tainted corn. It was Cassidy's anger that made her the perfect host, anger that I would later use to help her accept her Day of Remediation.

Cassidy immigrated to America along with millions of others. We survived the stench of human sweat and excrement in the holds of the ships meant to haul lumber. We landed in the filth and squalor of a New York tenement. Fourteen to a room. No toilet, no bath, no shower, no access to fresh air. The smell of sewer clinging to everything. Almost three hundred thousand people living in one square mile and signs in store windows that read: "Irish Need Not Apply."

When Cassidy's daughter, Grace, was born, Cassidy found salvation in the Mormons. She escaped the tenements and crossed the plains to find a home. Before the first shoots of Cassidy's potatoes had pushed themselves through the irrigated desert, she gave birth to a baby girl. Robins sang on her Day of Remediation four years later, leaving behind the 1853 yellow fever epidemic, my first successful copy of a master's creation.

The hotel work is hard but satisfying. We've been at it for three weeks, and Alicia has the routine down. We begin with rooms in disarray. When we leave, all is ordered, neat. Fresh towels and sheets. Pillows lined up on the beds. Glasses wrapped in paper. Alicia sees each room as a chance for a new beginning, as if by ordering the room she is ordering her life. But this thinking doesn't stop her from getting to work early so she can sweep through all the empty rooms looking for alcohol. Half-empty bottles of wine. Beer in the mini fridge. Once a bottle of scotch in a gift bag in the closet. Her previous conviction to stop drinking is forgotten.

Alicia takes advantage of the hotel and showers quickly every other day before she cleans the last bathroom of her room list. She works alone, uses her tip money to buy burgers and fries from Sam. She befriends Sam's eight-year-old son, Henry. She teaches him to play Crazy Eights with a pack of cards she took from a hotel room. I believe my instinct about Sam is correct, that one of my kind is patiently creating a gift for Sam's Day of Remediation. Maybe someday Henry will recreate my gift, just as I have recreated the gifts of other masters.

At the beginning of our fourth week, we leave work with a strong wind whipping seeds from the elms that line the old highway. The seeds rain down on us and swirl along the sidewalk, piling against the buildings like snowdrifts. When we get to the bar, Sam is outside with a broom in hand.

"I can sweep," Alicia says. "You've got customers." She gestures to a group of women wearing brightly colored tights and matching yellow jerseys. Alicia holds the broom in front of her self-consciously, as if to shield the faded T-shirt and jeans she has worn all month. The women walk into the bar between Alicia and Sam as if they are street posts.

"The bike race," Sam says. "They're starting to come. In a couple of days, the town will be filled. Competitors come from all over the country. All over."

Alicia imagines the places where the women might live. Places she might want to see. She has a seed of regret, thinking maybe she should have gone to Denver.

Regret I can work with.

When we get back to camp, two red-tailed hawks are circling above the cliffs.

Alicia takes out her bird handbook. She is becoming more receptive to my influence, and I now find her bird obsession useful. I direct her finger. *Red-tailed hawks are on a steady decline due to human persecution and habitat loss,* she reads.

As I hope, she thinks about persecution. She is far away from the persecution felt by Cassidy, but the seed of injustice is still there in her genetic memory, tied now to an abusive stepfather and a broken juvenile court system. She sits down and feels the cool grass through her jeans. She doesn't think about the grass, the way it bends beneath her, supporting her crushing weight, then slowly bounces back when she moves. Grass that is repeatedly cut but keeps growing. That is resilience. But Alicia is human, and the resilience of grass doesn't concern her.

A line of cars with bikes adorning their roofs like hunting trophies passes by. I understand now. Why we are here, and how Alicia's Day of Remediation will have an impact. Tourists. Tourists serve in the same way that the war served the Spanish Flu, a way to spread the virus quickly to many different places. Like the Spanish Flu, there will be no vaccine. I was true to the formula of each of the viruses I recreated in my hosts, faithful to the masters who preceded me. Now it is my turn.

I have no doubt that I am right, that Alicia's Day of Remediation is near. On the way to work today, her right leg starts to bend in places it shouldn't. She falls twice. By the time we get to work, her ankle aches and she is hesitant in her movements for fear of falling again. She finishes only half as many rooms as usual by noon. The head maid sends her home, saying that she isn't much help anyway. That Alicia looks a little green. I find humor in her statement. It is a human attribute, black humor. An attribute I have enjoyed with humans as my hosts.

Alicia sleeps well that night, partly my doing. We awaken to a finch call from the top of a cottonwood. The river has risen overnight, fed by melting mountain snow. The current spills over the stones along the beach. Alicia takes out her bird handbook, but she forgets what bird she means to find. She decides to take a walk, then forgets where she intends to go.

I direct her to a hillside strewn with smooth pebbles, remnants of a time when the river flowed at a higher level, curving next to the ship of sandstone that towers above us. When the river was this high, there might have been pine trees along the shore, or hummocks of sand that eventually were covered, compressed, then revealed as stone. There were no humans yet, but there were plants and animals. Plants and animals that exist only in the fossil record. I remind her of this. Of impermanence.

When Alicia reaches the edge of the canyon, she catches her breath at the view. A gorge of swirling ridges of striped stone that look like snakes. Farther in the distance, jagged towers of brown rocks stand like crowns above their regal domain. The canyon walls are striped with shades of cinnamon and white. Junipers slide their roots through cracks in the sandstone until they find water. Master survivors, junipers.

Alicia closes her eyes, opens them again, expects illusion has overtaken her sight. But the land is still there. The snakes. The crowns. In this moment, she feels she is seeing everything she might ever need to see. That if her sight is taken from her right now, she will not miss anything important.

I give her that message. I've begun to prepare her.

I've begun to prepare myself. She is my last. Six generations. Five times I reproduced what others created before me. This time, the gift will be my legacy. My mission will be over.

A wheeling mass of pinyon jays swoops past us. Alicia laughs. I give her this joy. It is the least I can do to thank her.

Pinyon jays called from tree to tree, claiming the boundary of their territory. Lillian, Alicia's great-grandmother, threw a pile of wood next to the fire pit, and the jays scattered. It was 1957, just one month before the first case of the Asian Flu in Utah. Lillian's daughter, Doris, had run off to be with a "slick talker." Lillian's words. Lillian moved into the hills around the farm where she grew up because she couldn't stand the confines of four walls. She blamed the walls for Doris's bad decision.

Lillian was nine when she became my host. It was after the Spanish Flu took fifty million people, her mother included. Lillian was strong-willed like her mother, and practical, but she was more interested in her internal world. Of all my hosts, Lillian and I were most alike, if such a comparison can be made.

Lillian's Day of Remediation came on the afternoon when we returned from the pinyon hills, smelling of campfire and grass and the sweet blossom of chokecherries. I was sorry to leave her. A human emotion, regret, but one I had come to know.

We walk back to camp through the scarred landscape of Sam's family's prison, the Japanese internment camp. Alicia sees the irreversible damage to the soil and the plant community. She hears their despair. She mingles the plants' voices with the heartbreak of the Japanese people. I count on this, of course. Empathy for others' suffering, be they plant or animal. This empathy helps my hosts see that there must be a culling, a cleansing. Otherwise, their Day of Remediation can be painful.

Alicia walks along the lines of the barracks, still visible in the soil, though the barracks have long since been relocated or destroyed. She climbs over the ruins of rock gardens created to add beauty where flowers could not grow. The subtle remains of cement board outline the barracks. The cement board was an attempt to provide protection from the wind-borne sand that permeated everything in the camp.

A van passes, pulls over to the side of the road. Bikes are fastened to the top of the roof. The driver gets out and sprays the road with two yellow arrows pointing to the cracked surface of the old highway. Arrows to direct the bikes as they race to the finish.

We will be there to greet them, Alicia and I, with our gift. My legacy.

A flock of goldfinches swirls in the direction of the arrows.

Tina, Alicia's mother, sat in a broken lawn chair in her living room. She watched a trio of goldfinches in her neighbor's bare-leafed plum tree. An episode of *Grey's Anatomy* was playing on the TV set. It was December 2007. Alicia's stepfather, Glen, was packing a paper bag with clothes from a laundry basket next to the kitchen table.

Five-year-old Alicia was under the table making herself small. She hugged her favorite stuffed toy, a floppy-eared dog named Puppy, close to her chest. She whispered into Puppy's ear. "Don't cry. It doesn't help if you cry."

Tina had streaks of tears on her cheeks, but she was calm now, enjoying the flight of birds out the window. The glass pipe that brought her this calm had fallen from her hand to the floor. Tina felt powerful, confident. And happy. A sense of joy that I could only liken to the joy flowers feel in the gaze of the sun. Tina had forgotten the event that led to her tears. She had also forgotten about Alicia. I tried to stop Tina from letting Glen take Alicia with him, but the meth made her immune to my influence.

Humans have a belief in something they call fairness, though what is thought fair varies widely from one individual to another. Two years later, on Tina's Day of Remediation, she was fifteen months clean and determined to find Alicia and prove herself fit to be in her daughter's life again. Maybe Tina's sacrifice was something humans would call unfair. Maybe I felt a bit this way at the time.

Sometimes, I am overcome with a sense that the state of the world is beyond remediation. With each host, I find much to tempt that way of thinking. Maybe that's why we are limited to six generations to achieve mastery. It might not be that our hosts' genetics lose their effectiveness, as we are taught to believe. It could just as well be that my kind become less capable of carrying out our mission as our focus becomes diluted with human ways of thinking. I admit it would be easier if I didn't remember each one of my hosts. If each new generation allowed me to start fresh, without the memory of the life taken. Still, I have done what needed to be done.

The humans claim something called pride, though what one person is proud of might be an atrocity to another. For us, the term may be more appropriately called accomplishment. Knowing we have achieved what we set out to do. I have chosen, for my last Day of Remediation, to return to the plant world. I was happiest when I lived among the flowers.

On her Day of Remediation, the day of the bike race, Alicia rises early while it is dark and the Milky Way is still a ribbon across the sky. She leaves without her shoes, and doesn't notice, not even when the sharp edges of the parking lot gravel cut into her feet. She has a sensation that her arms are curled like the tendrils of a fern.

When she crosses the thread of a stream running along the ditch, her right foot feels to her as if it disappears into a world beneath the sandy bottom. Once in town, her foot catches in a crack and she's sure her big toe snakes into the crack and holds her, just long enough to make her fall and barely miss landing face-first on the curb.

She isn't afraid, so I know she is receiving my calming messages, like whispers emanating from the wind, reassuring her. This is what needs to be done.

At the place where the bike racers must turn the corner around a narrow bend in the road, Alicia waits. The ground tells her why she has come. It calls to her to help remediate what humans have done to themselves. A cleansing to allow them to regroup and try again. We try only to assist them. Reduce their populations. Hope for a better future.

I help Alicia find this understanding, turn the steel of her anger into strength. I remind her of the lost plants, the extinct birds, the persecution of humans. She allows her feet to narrow, to elongate and dig deep into the earth.

And then she resists.

I can feel Alicia's pain. I try to help her see that there is only pain in her future, that this day will end that pain. Give her the music of flowers. Give her a place to call home after never having one. Take away the battle with alcohol.

But still she resists.

I remind her that my kind have been around since life began. We depend on life, but life also depends on us. Humans say we infect plants and animals. They call us a parasite, unable to replicate without a host. They are oblivious to our powers. Abilities beyond any they might understand. We are our own kingdom, battling to save life with the viruses we create, not to take it.

I remind Alicia of her history. Her stepfather, her mother, her life in foster care and detention. All the people who turned their back on her. Injustice. Persecution. I echo those words in her ear, reaching for the genetic memory going all the way back to that windy day in Ireland in 1847.

Finally, Alicia relaxes. She doesn't cry out when her eyes close permanently and her arms split apart into many thin branches with ready-to-burst blossoms.

My gift is there. In the pollen of the flowers. Ready.

The lead bikers are red-faced and serious. Their muscled legs pump the pedals past us. They are breathing hard, and my pollen moves easily into their lungs. My new virus, alive in each grain. The bikers pedal on, knowing nothing of their silent gift. Another string of bikers, and another. Enough pollen for all, until the last of the riders have turned the narrow corner around the colorful bush that they wouldn't have seen the day before.

Two weeks. Then the symptoms will appear. Highly contagious. Resistant. I hope for the same success as HIV.

It is quiet here on the hill. Twice a day, a train passes by, but it doesn't stop. Summer comes, then fall, then winter, then spring again. And Alicia and I sing.

Prior to becoming an educator, B.J. Eardley worked a variety of jobs including counselor, organic farmer, bookkeeper, travel agent, and tour guide. As a freelance writer, she published feature articles on the cultural and natural history of southeastern Utah, where she lives. To appease the voices in her head, she is currently focused on historical and speculative fiction. She began "Remediation" by putting a character from a previous short story on a train with a mysterious companion. Who that companion turned out to be was a complete surprise.

FAIRE-WEATHER MAGIC

by Kendra Merritt

As long as she kept them laughing, the joke was on them. As long as they were laughing, they wouldn't notice anything wrong with her spells.

Unless something blew up.

Livia pushed her sleeves up with a flourish, then showed her hands to the crowd. *Don't explode, don't explode, don't explode*, she chanted in the back of her mind. Then aloud she whispered the levitation spell. A man in the crowd jumped as his top hat rose and floated toward her.

"Ladies and gentlemen," Livia said in her best stage voice. Her crowd wasn't particularly large, but it was best to play it as though she spoke to a packed theater rather than a bustling side street. "Hang on to your hats. Things have a tendency to wander off around here."

Someone was grilling sausages down the way, and the smell of popped corn made her stomach growl. Liv reminded it that she could eat after she'd earned enough coin to feed Ren. Ren always came first.

The crowd laughed as the man lunged for his hat. It spun away, brushing the strands of second-rate mage globes strung overhead.

"Let me help you with that, sir," Liv said, then made a theatrical leap for the floating hat.

She wore the tailored suit and hat of a gentleman deliberately. First, because it made her look older. And second, because if people looked at her and saw a girl masquerading as a man, they assumed that was the only gimmick, and they didn't look for any deeper secrets. They wouldn't ask to see her mage license or examine it closely enough to notice it was a forgery.

As her fingers touched the hat, the black satin curled back and squawked at her. A big black crow flapped its wings and dove over the crowd.

Uh, that wasn't supposed to happen. She scanned the crowd, but she didn't see the bald head of the Redundancy Bureau rep she'd come to know and avoid. Her shoulders relaxed just a smidge.

All right, illusions it is.

Several of the men laughed as they ducked away from the crow, and a couple ladies shrieked and raised their gloved hands to protect their heads.

Liv jumped after the crow, scrambling to pull together another spell on the fly. As she passed through the crowd, another man's hat flew away squawking. And another. Soon the air was filled with flapping impossibilities. The crowd roared with laughter and dove for their hats while Liv kept the tight smile plastered across her face.

Glimmers of vytl, the magical energy harnessed by spells, flitted through the air. Vytl that Liv shouldn't be able to see. One of the mage globes overhead popped and shattered. The sound made Liv flinch.

That's enough of that. Better end it now, while everyone is still intact.

Liv cut off the ends of her spell just in time to catch the first crow as it passed. The bird disappeared in a shower of sparks and an undignified squawk, revealing the illusion for what it was. She handed the man back his hat.

"Sorry about that," she said with a mischievous grin.

One by one, she grabbed the errant apparel and returned it to its owners as they laughed and clapped for what seemed like a well-done piece of magic.

It hadn't been the set she'd planned on, but on the bright side, nothing had exploded yet—if you didn't count the mage globe. And the coins showering the cobbles at her feet would buy Ren's dinner tonight with some left over for a cake or two.

Liv smiled.

In that moment of satisfaction, streaks of vytl unbound by a spell smeared her vision, cutting across the last illusion. The sparks closed in on her and swirled around her sleeves.

Her cuffs burst into flame.

Liv shouted and waved her arms in a dissipation spell, but the fire licked up the fabric, as if searching for her.

Muck in a saint's handbasket, Ren will never let me hear the end of it if I go up in flames on the street.

Ignoring propriety, she stripped out of her jacket. As she dropped the garment, the flames surged upward and engulfed the cheap black wool, leaving nothing but a pile of ash on the cobbles.

Liv's chest heaved as she scanned the crowd. Her audience blinked in confusion, murmuring questions to each other.

"Was that supposed to happen?"

"That didn't look like a sanctioned spell to me."

"Should we report it?"

Liv chewed her lip. The representative might not have been there to catch her mistake, but the crowd certainly wasn't stupid. She wove together a new illusion, being careful to stick with easily recognized spells, ones that everyone knew were sanctioned by the Redundancy Bureau. She twirled as another coat appeared to cover her shirt, and she bowed with a theatrical flourish.

The crowd broke into cheers, accepting the final trick with only a moment's hesitation.

Liv gave her audience a rueful grin as they applauded, hiding the way her heart beat in her throat. She was lucky, so very lucky, they'd thought it was all part of the show. Practicing magecraft without a license was only the first of her offenses. No matter how much she tried to stick with sanctioned spells, something always went wrong. And unsanctioned magic was illegal in all twelve duchies. It would bring the Bureau down on her and Ren faster than a crashing airship. And after that, prison.

Fortunately, everyone knew that spells were tightly regulated by the Bureau. The same way everyone knew that mages could only access vytl through spells. Yes, there were enchanters, who supposedly saw and controlled vytl themselves, but since there was only one of those in the whole world right now, no one would readily guess just how many laws Liv was breaking.

Too bad Liv's magic didn't seem to care about following any of the rules. Spells always seemed to go sideways for her, and things tended to explode when she got angry or nervous. But only another mage would recognize that her spells didn't follow any of the Bureau's rules. She'd be safe as long as no one with a license showed up.

Gentlemen offered their arms and led their ladies away toward the rest of the faire, their skirts sweeping the cobbles, as Liv knelt and gathered the coins around her feet. She scooped them deftly into her trouser pockets and jerked her head to blow long red hair out of her face. She used to have an assistant for this sort of thing, but the girl had run off after one too many explosions.

Liv started to stand, then froze.

Just a few feet away, where the crowd had been moments before, sat a young woman. Her narrow hands rested on the wheels of a strange chair. It rolled along the cobbles as if the woman couldn't use her own legs. The curly brown hair draped over her shoulder didn't quite hide the symbol of a licensed mage pinned to her gown.

The woman's hazel eyes narrowed as she regarded Liv, and Liv flushed in the patchy light of the faire.

Oh, muck.

This wasn't the normal Bureau rep. But she was staring at Liv as if she'd seen the misbehaving vytl. There was no way she'd missed the illusions that hadn't come from a sanctioned spell. Any moment now she'd ask to see Liv's license, and it would all be over. The forgery was good enough to fool the officers who issued the street faire's permit, but it wouldn't withstand closer scrutiny from a mage.

The woman pushed the wheels of her chair and rolled forward across the cobbles.

Liv didn't doubt that this woman was fully capable of hunting her down, wheeled chair or not. In two seconds flat, Liv disappeared into the crowd, putting as many bodies between her and the strange woman as possible. Those wheels might have been able to keep up on a clear street, but the mage would have to navigate around and through the press of people. And Liv knew the secrets of slipping through a crowd. The faire had been her home for three years, after all.

Liv threaded through the booths, passing the faire-master as he enticed passers-by into the depths of the faire with promises of entertainment and fried food. She ducked her head when he looked her way. The man had no problem employing mages with less-than-perfect credentials. But those other mages didn't have bits of unbound vytl following them around like stray cats who knocked over the milk.

A rangy dog with wiry gray hair whined in the open mouth of an alley. Liv spared him a glance and slowed. Then she sighed and fished in her pockets for something more substantial than coins. All that met her fingers were a couple pieces of candy and some lint. She pulled out a piece of taffy and tossed it to the dog, then moved on.

"What is this, candy? I've heard it's not very good for you." Someone licked their lips behind her. "Ommph, it's sweet. And sticky."

She whirled around to see the dog chewing industriously. No one else had stopped to stare at him in horror, but she could have sworn she'd heard him speak. The dog's tail thumped the cobblestones.

Liv shook her head. No. Either she'd been imagining it or the unsanctioned magic was getting worse. Could she have cast some sort of sound illusion without even realizing it?

She turned to leave the problem behind but stopped short. At the end of the street, the woman in the chair sat scanning the crowd.

She must have gone around on a clearer street.

Liv sucked in a breath and spun on her heel, plunging back into the crowd. She dropped the illusion of her jacket, hoping it would change her appearance enough to throw off the mage.

She was such an idiot. She'd thought the street faire was the perfect place to hide the occasional burst of an unsanctioned spell. Hiding the very real but very illegal magic amongst the gaudy fakery seemed like hiding a priceless necklace amongst costume jewelry. Plain sight and all that.

But that shield seemed false and flimsy now, with a real mage rolling up behind her.

Liv passed a booth selling sparklers and glittering mage globes you could hold in your hand. Vytl zipped past her in bands and waves, and one by one the sparklers all lit up, sending hot embers out to sting the vendor's bare hands.

An animal yelped, and Liv looked back to see the dog slinking along behind her.

That's what she got for feeding the poor thing, but she did not have time to deal with a stray who may or may not have a voice of his own.

"Go on," she said, waving her hands at the dog. "Go home. I don't deal with talking dogs."

"Not even if I can help you?" The mongrel stopped in the middle of the flow of traffic and sat on his haunches. "I have a wide range of skills, from fierce guardian to just looking cute." He whined again and gazed up at her with bright blue eyes.

Liv pressed her hands to her temples. "This cannot be happening." Luckily the faire was too noisy for anyone to notice her own personal demon. Or maybe she really had dreamed him up.

A mage globe on the stand beside them shattered, making the vendor swear. Liv fought to calm her racing heart. She was losing control.

Muck, who was she kidding? She'd lost control a while ago. All she did now was smile and pretend everything was all right.

"Just stay away from me," Liv said to the dog. "Either you're a figment of my imagination or you're a spell gone bad. And I don't want the Bureau coming in to find out which one."

With their parents gone, she was the only one around to take care of Ren. She couldn't afford to be arrested. But she also couldn't afford the time or money to go to the University and get her license for real.

Liv's jaw clenched and she hurried off, leaving the dog behind. Several booths down she raised her gaze, searching for a short blond head in the chaos of the faire.

"Sour taffy!" a high, clear voice called above the general hubbub. "Sweet caramel, anyone want sweet caramel?"

Liv smiled and headed for the voice.

A ten-year-old boy stood on an empty crate, singing out, "Candy, three bits a bag!" His strawberry-blond hair glinted in the light of the mage globes as he grinned at the faire-goers.

"Ren," Liv said, taking his arm. "Time to go."

"My shift's not over for another fifteen minutes," Ren said, but he stepped down off the crate anyway.

"I know, but something's come up. We have to get out of sight for a while."

She set off down the row of booths and Ren trotted to keep up, his tray of candy held carefully between his hands. "What's wrong?" he said. "Wait, did you muck up a spell again?" He gave her a cheeky grin.

"Language," Liv said.

"What? Muck? Oh, come on. Everybody says it."

"You're not everybody. You're my little brother, and I say you're too young to swear."

"We're not talking about me," he said, skipping ahead of her to walk backward, wending through the crowd like a fish through seaweed. "We're talking about your mucked-up spell. What did you set fire to this time?"

"Nothing." Liv winced.

"Is that why you're not wearing a jacket?" Ren guffawed when she didn't answer.

"It's not funny. It's serious. We have to lay low so the Bureau doesn't come after us."

"You mean, so they don't come after *you*. But why now? You've messed up spells before. What's different this time?"

"Someone saw."

He frowned but for once didn't have anything to say. He slid the lid onto his box of candy and tucked it under his arm, then sprinted ahead of her. He might tease her, but he knew the consequences if she was caught as well as she did. He'd lost enough people in his young life; he didn't need to lose her, too.

He ducked between a couple booths and through the ratty curtain that hid their private space from the rest of the faire. The back walls of the booths formed a triangle with enough room for two hammocks and a cook-pot. Most nights there was even food to put in it.

Hard to believe this was a huge step up from where they'd been the first few months after Papa died. Liv snagged Ren's arm to give him a quick, fierce hug, shying away from the memories of those nights filled with hunger and fear and worry. She'd kept Ren alive and well, and that was all she wanted to remember about that time.

Ren made a disgusted noise and pulled away from her embrace. She squeezed one more time to make sure he knew she was the boss before releasing him.

"So, what happened this time?" Ren asked seriously as he settled into his hammock.

Liv took off her top hat and hung it on a post with a sigh. "Some vytl got in the way. It's like it's attracted to me somehow. It won't stop interfering with my spells."

"I don't understand what the big deal is. Don't those enchanters use vytl without spells all the time?"

She shook her head in frustration, trying to remember that Ren had been only seven when their parents died. He hadn't absorbed nearly as many of Papa's stories and lessons about mages and enchanters.

"There's only one of those. Lady Marion Hode. And there's only one because no one really knows how she became an enchanter."

"You'd think she'd know."

"She's said it had something to do with trauma. But that doesn't help me. I'm not some kind of enchanter.

I'm just a mage without a license, and some rogue vytl thinks I'm interesting."

"Doesn't the Bureau have more important things to do than tracking down one unlicensed mage?"

"Stories about mages who play with unlicensed magic always end badly," she said. "It's dangerous. You've seen how dangerous."

"I guess they don't want anyone blowing up their city when they break the rules."

"Minimum sentence of ten years," Liv said quietly. "But that won't happen. I'll learn how to control this."

"That's good to hear," a rumbly voice said from behind them. "Then I won't have to throw you out."

Liv straightened and turned to face the faire-master, who stood in the slim opening of their space. His broad frame dwarfed their squalid home. He wore a bright green suit and matching top hat, designed to attract attention, unlike Liv's dusty black, designed to be overlooked.

"Sir," Liv said. "I can explain."

"You can explain how a licensed mage found you in my street faire?"

Liv's mouth fell open, then she closed it with a snap. "The one in the chair?"

"Says she's investigating unsanctioned spells. Got anything you want to tell me?"

Liv's throat bobbed as she swallowed. "It was an accident, sir."

"Liv just has the kind of talent that sets things on fire," Ren said.

Liv scowled at him.

The faire-master lifted his hat and ran a hand through his greased hair. "Look, most of this operation is aboveboard. But I can't have you drawing attention to yourself. I lied for you this once. I told the mage that you were licensed with all the proper paperwork. But you have to control this…" He waved a hand at her vaguely. "Whatever this is. A little theft, a little forgery, those I can get away with. But unsanctioned spells? That's trouble I can't afford. It'll shut the whole faire down for sure. Control it, or I'll kick you so far out of this faire, you'll land in the harbor. Both of you."

"Yes, sir!" Ren said with a mock military salute.

Liv gripped his arm and gave him a threatening look. Then she turned back to the faire-master. "It won't happen again, sir. I promise."

It couldn't happen again. Not if she wanted to keep Ren safe and happy. The faire was their home, and the faire-master was the only one standing between them and the Bureau.

He gave her a narrow-eyed look and spun away, letting their curtain swish shut behind him.

Liv sighed, shoulders sagging. She collapsed into one of the hammocks, letting it swing. Silent for once, Ren came to lean against her. He reached in his pocket and handed her a piece of taffy, his lips pressed thin. The familiar ritual made her eyes sting, and she reached out automatically to take the candy. The tradition had been around since that first year on the street, when he'd found her crying from the weight of it all but was too young to know how to tell her it would be all right.

It was Ren's way of saying he trusted her. He trusted her to do the right thing for the two of them. Even when all the evidence pointed to the contrary.

The next night, Liv made sure to set herself up on a corner closer to Ren. She could keep an eye on him and be close enough to grab him in case the Bureau rep came back and they had to flee.

While he grinned and cajoled passing customers into buying candy, Liv twisted her fingers, sending a bit of wind to lift and twirl seven paper birds she'd scattered on the ground before her. She carefully stuck to well-known, recognizable spells today, ignoring the flits and flashes of unbound vytl around her. It streamed past her in smears of color and whispers of power.

You can't see vytl, her father's voice said in her head. *You can't touch it. Only the effects of a spell can be seen. Vytl has to be bound by a spell; it's a law of nature. Even the mages at the University haven't come up with a way to see it.*

Her paper birds fluttered and twitched like real creatures as she made them dance for the crowd. Sweat dampened the inside of her top hat, but she pasted a confident grin on her face.

Keep smiling, keep them laughing, and no one will look any closer.

The crowd tittered as her birds flitted among them, tugging gently at shawls and hems. One alighted on a lady's shoulder and trilled.

That was more complicated. Liv wove the sound illusion with her left hand while her right kept the movement spells going. No rogue vytl here. Only honest, hard-working spells.

Three boys raced past, waving sparklers. She shook her head, familiar with the antics of kids stuffed with too much cotton candy. She reached out to de-spell her birds.

A loud bang and the shatter of glass made her jump. It took only a split second for her to realize where the noise came from—the boys had knocked over a popcorn vendor's cart just down the row—but it still made her heart pound.

Ribbons of red and gold vytl streaked toward her as if responding to her fear. Their usual gentle hum turned into a shriek as they split the air and collided before her.

The paper birds shot into the sky, circled once, then dove for the faire patrons.

Liv gaped as ladies screamed and their gentlemen chased tiny homicidal birds around the street. She raised her hands to cut off the spell that kept them moving and promptly realized she wasn't in control. The birds had taken in the rogue vytl and now moved with a life of their own.

Ren stood on his box across the cobblestones, laughing so hard his hat had fallen off.

Liv raced through the chaos trying to catch the birds. She managed to snatch one between her palms, and it gave a distressed cheep before she crumpled it and stuffed it in her pocket. As the crowd scattered in panic, she leapt for each bird, praying she caught them all before one of them paper-cut someone to death.

Beside her, a tall, gray dog jumped after the birds, snatching them between his teeth and shaking them into submission.

Liv caught the last bird and ducked into an alley to crumple up all the little paper corpses. One wing fluttered in the breeze, and she crushed it ruthlessly.

"Were they supposed to act like that?"

Liv gasped and started so badly she nearly fell over. She put a hand to the slimy wall to steady herself and whipped around.

The empty alley stared back at her. Empty except for the gray dog. His tail thumped as he blinked bright blue eyes.

Not again.

"Is anyone there?" she said, hoping desperately that someone would answer. Someone human.

The dog cocked its head. "You're looking right at me. Can you not see me? Did I become invisible somehow?"

Liv dropped the wad of paper and buried her face in her hands with a groan.

A wet tongue swiped her knuckles and the exposed bits of her face. "You don't look so good. Are you ill?"

She made a face and pushed against the wiry hair on his chest. "Stop that. I don't know if anyone's told you, but talking dogs are kind of creepy."

The dog sat back on his haunches and sighed. "I get that all the time. But I assure you, where I come from, it's quite common."

Liv's brow furrowed as she thought through all of Papa's lessons. Had he said anything about giving voice to other creatures? No, but he'd mentioned Marion Hode, who studied the other realms that paralleled theirs. And there were mages at the University who could summon creatures across the borders. *They look like beasts but have the intelligence and wit of humans*, Papa had said.

Her hands crept to her mouth. If she thought a couple unsanctioned spells were bad, summoning a creature like this without a license was even worse.

"Muck on me, did I call you by accident?" This was exactly why the Bureau was so hard on unlicensed mages. So things like this didn't happen. What if this creature attracted their attention? They'd swoop in here, clear out the street faire, and take her away from Ren. He'd be out on the street for the second time in his young life—only this time, she wouldn't be there to protect him.

"Get out of here," she said, waving her hands and startling the dog enough to make him back up. "Shoo. Go back to where you came from."

There had to be a way to unsummon something from this realm, but if there was, she didn't know it. She couldn't do anything except distance herself and Ren.

She stamped her foot and yelled, "Scat!"

The dog darted to the other end of the alley, then stopped to give her a hurt look.

"Don't look at me like that. You're the one who doesn't belong here." She turned and rushed toward the lights of the faire, looking for Ren. Leaving behind the creature that would only serve as a beacon for the Bureau.

The faire moved every fortnight, on a regular circuit with five locations in the city and twenty scattered around the countryside. Liv managed to convince the faire-master to move them early this time, arguing that it would be harder for the mage to find her—not to mention the persistent dog.

They were so practiced that it only took them a day to move the faire from the cross street to a market square near the east gate of the city. Farmers' markets occupied the square in the summer and fall, but it stood empty in the spring until they moved in.

As Liv helped hang strings of mage globes across the space, she cast a glance toward the main street. No gray dogs or mages in wheeled chairs. Maybe the move had foiled all the strangers following her. And surely once they left the city she'd be safe from any prying mages or Bureau representatives. They wouldn't follow one dysfunctional spell caster into the countryside. Would they?

Liv passed the strand of mage globes through her hands, finding a couple that flickered weakly. She began drawing the pieces of a recharging spell together.

A broad hand came down on her wrists. The faire-master's bushy black eyebrows drew together. "No magic. Not for little things," he said. "It goes wrong around you too often. Stick to the illusions and tricks for the show."

Liv flushed, her face stinging in the dim light of sunset. "Yes, sir," she mumbled.

If the faire-master was worried enough to keep her from casting everyday spells, how long before he decided she was a risk and kicked her and Ren out completely? With no place to sleep and no job, they'd be back to those early days when she'd had to dig through trash heaps to feed them.

Liv stalked off to find Ren, hands clenched in her pockets. They had appropriated a spot at the dead end of an alley, where they could hang their hammocks between the two walls. With a threadbare curtain strung across the opening, it afforded a modicum of privacy.

The murmur of voices made her frown as she pushed past the curtain.

Ren sat sharing a muffin with a big, gray dog with bright blue eyes.

Liv sucked in a breath. The dog had found her. Across the city it had tracked her, and now it sat here grinning as if it weren't threatening her livelihood—and worse, her family.

Ren bounced to his feet, leaving the muffin in crumbs on the cobblestones. "Hey look, Liv. The dog talks."

Liv snatched Ren's shoulders to draw him closer to her. "What are you doing here?" she said to the dog, who sat with his tongue lolling. "Stay away from my brother. You'll bring the Bureau down on us. You'll put him in danger, too."

"Zev doesn't have anything to do with the Bureau," a voice said behind Liv. "The only one he'll be bringing here is me."

Liv gasped and whirled around to see the woman in the wheeled chair push aside their curtain. The mage's pin glinted from the shoulder of her dress.

Liv glared at the dog. "You're working together."

He panted unapologetically. "You're trapped now. Can't get away from us."

Panic surged in Liv's chest. He was right. The dead-end alley, which had seemed so comforting before, was now a cage to keep them from running.

She was going to jail. That was for sure. Her fingers tightened on Ren's shoulders, as if that would make any difference. As if she could anchor her pounding heart to his and keep them together through anything.

Streams of vytl speared toward her in a whirlwind of color and sound. It rushed past her ears, making her flinch. The sparks of vytl collided, setting fire to the air around her.

Flames burst out from her, dancing across the open space to lick at the hammocks and the curtain. Liv flung her arms around Ren and tried to shield him with her body as heat beat at her face and exposed hands. His arms tightened around her middle, pinching her too hard, but she welcomed that pain compared to the flames.

Fire raced across the cobbles, jumping the spaces where it had nothing to burn, and headed for the rest of the faire.

Water, they needed water. Or a dissipation spell. Liv thrust Ren behind her and stretched out stinging fingers to form the spell. But when she tried to speak the words, acrid smoke burned her throat and she doubled over, coughing.

Whispers against her ears made her shake her head. She peered through the conflagration, eyes streaming, following the sound of vytl. The Bureau mage and the dog sat calmly in the center of the firestorm, eyes on Liv and her brother. The flames circled her, leaving a space of clear air where the vytl swirled around her in smooth, ordered eddies.

The woman didn't raise her hands or her voice in a spell. But the vytl sought her out, centering on her in little rivers and pools. As if it was attracted to her.

Just like it did with Liv.

Liv straightened, leaving Ren's arms around her middle. *She's like me. But she can control it. It can be controlled.* Along with the thought, the knot in Liv's chest released, a wash of relief making her knees shake.

Using the woman's example as a guide, Liv pulled the vytl in the flames around her into neat, ordered rows. It had always reacted to her fear and anger, but this time it reacted to her calm. She forced the bits of vytl straight and pulled the power out of the fire, making it flicker and die.

Leaving them in an alley darkened with twilight that smelled like scorched stone and burnt muffin.

The dog whined and said, "I take it I frightened them?"

"Good guess," the woman said. "Probably shouldn't have pointed out they were trapped."

"I always manage to say the wrong thing. Humans are so complicated."

Liv peered around the alley, body trembling. Weak strands of vytl straggled through the air, but this time they weren't heading for Liv. They gathered around the woman in the chair, circling her and ordering themselves into neat rows and streams, then they settled calmly into the cobbles at her feet, as if waiting to be called.

"You didn't use a spell," Liv said, voice hoarse against the silence.

"No," the woman said.

"You're…you're like me."

The sound of pounding feet made Liv's fingers clench on Ren's shoulders again. The faire-master pushed through the blackened rags that had once been their curtain, face red and eyes livid.

"That is it, Liv. Don't bother packing up. I want you and your brother out now."

"Wait, no. Please," Liv said, stepping forward. "We have nowhere else to go."

"See if I care," the faire-master said. "I can't afford for a Bureau mage to show up—"

"Too late," the woman in the chair said, catching the faire-master's attention.

He spluttered. "Mistress, I didn't see you."

"Clearly."

"Was anyone hurt?" Liv asked before he could demand the mage haul her away to prison.

The faire-master's lips went thin, but he shook his head. "No, the fire stopped at the end of the alley. Like it hit a wall. I've never seen a spell like that."

"That's because it wasn't a spell. It was me," the mage said. She glanced at Liv. "I knew cornering you might be a bad idea, but I couldn't see any other way. So I was ready."

The faire-master threw up his hands. "More unsanctioned magic?"

The woman shot a scathing glance at him. "Go sputter somewhere else, if you can't keep from interrupting me."

The faire-master's mouth fell open, and Liv choked on a laugh.

"Unsanctioned magic actually protected people?" Liv said. "But mine's always just caused trouble."

The woman huffed a laugh. "This isn't unsanctioned magic, just untamed. At least in your case. The Bureau doesn't exactly like what I can do, but they were quick to agree when I offered to help find other enchanters."

Liv collapsed against the wall. "You're Lady Marion Hode. The only enchanter in the world."

"Not anymore," Marion said.

Liv's mouth went dry when she realized what Lady Marion was saying. "No. I mean, I'm just unlicensed. That's why my spells go wrong. I haven't had the training." She bit her lip and plowed on, trying to explain. "Enchanters have to have something bad happen to them, don't they? They have some sort of trauma." She stopped herself from gesturing to the woman's legs, realizing how rude that would be.

But Lady Marion's lips twisted in a self-deprecating grin, as if she knew exactly what Liv was thinking. "Yes," she said. "Our strength comes from everything we've lived through. It comes from surviving. But not every trauma is physical." She tilted her head.

Liv opened her mouth to deny it, but she stopped at the memories of those days after Mama and Papa died. Huddled in an alley trying to keep Ren warm. Endless grief and worry gnawing at the back of her mind. Promising Ren she'd never let him be hungry or cold or afraid again, not knowing if she'd be able to keep that promise.

"Did you have spells that exploded, too?" Liv asked. "Fires that started for no reason, winds that knocked people over?"

"Mine weren't as spectacular as yours," the enchanter said. "Maybe because I wasn't trying so hard to hide it."

"There's no way this is legal," the faire-master said, reminding both Lady Marion and Liv that he was still there. "Just letting untrained enchanters roam the city, setting fire to everything."

Lady Marion's eyes flashed. "Maybe you'd like to tell me how to do my job better. No one's ever done this before, but of course, you must have loads of experience."

The dog stood and stretched, then used his narrow head to nudge the faire-master toward the alley opening. "That's your cue to leave. Trust me, you won't win any arguments against Merry. Her wits—and her tongue—are sharper than yours."

"So are you going to take us with you?" Ren asked the enchanter as the faire-master was herded down the alley. "Do we get to live in a tower?"

Lady Marion raised an eyebrow. "I mostly live in my office. But you can have a room at the University. Your sister will have to choose." She pinned Liv with her glance. "You can stay here and work with that buffoon—" She gestured at the faire-master's retreating back. "—trying not to set fire to the city. Or you can come help me figure out how to be both a mage and an enchanter. It's a wide-open field at the moment."

Liv gulped. Put like that, the choice seemed simple, but there were other things to think about...

She glanced at Ren.

He stood on the scorched cobblestones, his hand already digging in his pocket. As if he knew what was going through her head. He pulled his hand out and offered something to her.

Her breath caught and she met his eyes. He gave her his biggest grin.

She took the taffy and rolled it between her fingers, the wax paper smooth and familiar to her fingertips.

She finally looked up at Lady Marion. "I did always want to go to the University."

———————————

Books have been Kendra Merritt's escape for as long as she can remember. She used to hide fantasy novels behind her government textbook in high school, and she wrote most of her first novel during a semester of college algebra.

Older and wiser now (but just as nerdy), she writes retellings of fairy tales with main characters who have disabilities. If she's not writing, she's reading, and if she's not reading, she's playing video games. She lives in Denver with her very tall husband, their book-loving progeny, and a lazy black monster masquerading as a service dog.

"Faire-Weather Magic" is a part of the Mark of the Least *series, where Kendra tells familiar stories from unfamiliar points of view.*

SCHRÖDINGER'S MOUSE

by Amy Drayer

I spent that morning harried by a small bee. The buzz got in my head, became one of those noises that make up the fabric of everything, so you don't notice it until it stops. Finally, the bee landed on the table beside me. I folded the newspaper I'd just finished and swatted it. Nothing personal, just that my wife is allergic. It's habit now. I was glad it wasn't a fat fuzzy bumbler. I like those.

I scraped the remains off the table with the paper. With the tip of my shoe I nudged the body through the cracks of the deck. Bees can still get you, after you kill them. The stinger's still there—someone steps on it, your dog eats it, you don't know what could happen.

"You want more coffee?" My wife poked her head out the screen door, pot in hand, still sporting pajamas and bed head. Can you beat lazy Sunday mornings? No, you cannot. Now that neither of us had papers to grade on the weekend, we were starting to have a hard time knowing what to do with ourselves. The languor was glorious.

"Yeah. I'm coming in. It's too hot out here." Summer-hot and uncomfortable and I resented that. Retirement was supposed to be twenty-four-seven, wall-to-wall leisure. We'd just started that part of our journey together. It was good, but there were a lot of promises that weren't paying off.

Inside, it was cool. I felt a little rush of ambition and decided to finish off the breakfast dishes. I opened the kitchen cupboard below the sink, bent down to grab the dish soap, and froze with my hand mid-grab. At the back of the cabinet, on one of the sticky pads the exterminator had left last week, was a live mouse.

"Dammit." I'd had misgivings, ideas about this particular development when we'd left the sticky traps. But we were tired of finding tiny rodent craps all over the kitchen.

"What's up?" my wife called from the living room.

"Nothing, hon."

Jean's tender-hearted. Not in a saccharine way—only she's one of those people you don't like to tell sickly things to, in the same way you wouldn't want to tell your grandmother in detail how women smuggle heroin across borders. There's no point to it.

The whiskers on the mouse's nose twitched as he poked his slender gray head toward the light. He—or she, I didn't know, and it wasn't like I was going to check—wasn't alarmed by the sight of me. Silent, he seemed to ask with mild black eyes, "Hey there, could you help me out? I can't seem to get free." The tail was stuck completely to the pale-yellow pad, and all four tiny paws. He wasn't panicked. Yet. Only confused. He had not yet begun to imagine the worst. Do mice have imagination? Or do they skip the existential terror of death? And is that lack of self-awareness better than wringing his pink paws over leaving his nest and children behind, worrying about whether Aunt Joan and his mother will get along at the service?

I walked into the dining room. "There's a live mouse on one of the traps." The horror of my discovery overwhelmed my desire to shield my wife from the unpleasantries of rural life. And Jean's always been tougher than I gave her credit for.

"Oh God." She opened her mouth, then closed it, grimaced. "Oh no."

"I know."

We stared at each other. Jean was perfectly capable of handling some of the uglier household chores that came down the pipe—fishing dead birds out of the little pond in the back, for instance—but the understanding was that if I was around, I got the short straw. The rule hadn't been declared one day; we'd simply silently negotiated this and so many other arrangements over the last twenty years.

Perhaps, ultimately, it's because I'm a carnivore and she's not. Dead animals fall squarely in my purview. Or, in this case, animals that are about to be dead.

"What should we do?" she asked. This was the royal we, of course. She meant, what would I do?

"We can't just wait for it to die," I replied.

Here we were, square at the heart of the matter. We'd already killed the mouse. Now we were just wringing our hands about *how* it was going to make its final exit. How cruel would we be? I certainly don't have antipathy toward rodents. As a kid I had gerbils. They became quite friendly. I'd pet them and spend time chatting with them. I bred them a few times, watched the pink-brown quivering blobs grow to develop eyes and hair and curiosity. Inevitably, one would chew through the brightly colored plastic adventure tubes that formed a web of civilization throughout my bedroom. I'd hunt for them for hours in the dusty attic and assorted dark corners of the home, and I never found one. We had cats, too.

My wife only looked at me, then went back to her book. I went back into the kitchen. I had to look again. This decision couldn't be made without a more thorough assessment of the life in question. I hadn't noticed much about the little guy under there. Getting closer to it all would help me make up my mind about what came next.

Next couldn't be walking out of the house, going to the grocery store, coming home, cooking dinner, going to bed. No. We couldn't simply go about our lives as the critter suffered and waited to die. Or, as we waited for him to die. How long would it take if we just let the thing linger? Dehydration would get it, eventually. It takes seven days for a human to die without water, right? How long for a mouse?

I opened the cupboard again and sighed, grabbed the soap. Mouse or no, I needed to run the dishwasher yet again, because there was a moldy smell to it. We'd been down in Mexico most of the winter, so every time you opened the damn thing rot assailed you bodily.

I fired up the washer and returned to the question at hand. There was no way to get him off the trap. It would rip the skin right off, and I'd probably catch some fatal mouse-bite illness if I tried. I wasn't going to stuff him in a trash bag and wait for him to suffocate. And I couldn't just toss the whole problem outside and wait for the circle of life to right my wrong. What else might stick a beak or a paw or a scale on the glue? Soon enough we'd have a menagerie of wildlife waiting out their fates—

"Is this how you expected it to end, Snake?"

"Why no, Field Hawk, it's not."

"Can someone please just tell me what's going on?" the mouse might add.

When Bill from The Rat Detective had come around, I'd hemmed and hawed about the sticky pads. Eventually, I decided the most likely outcome would be that I'd waltz in one morning and something ugly would be desiccated and dead under the sink. I'd throw it in the garbage, take the garbage outside, place the bag in the bin and that would be that.

My lack of imagination had been staggering, and ultimately, ironic.

The mouse still offered very little reaction to my appearance. He did seem more subdued, still glancing around, nose working the air, but acclimating to me. Was he dying already? I could only hope. Perhaps he would have a mouse heart attack and considerately resolve my dilemma. Instead, he continued his visual and olfactory inspection of the world. He had no way to move at all, no way to change his situation, absolutely no control over anything. He ought to be frenzied. Maybe that part would come later, as worry over a dry mouth and empty stomach turned to sick unease, and then to terror. But then again, maybe those are emotions beyond mouse capacity.

From the dining room, my wife again: "You could drown it. It's how my dad used to do it."

Now I pictured the guy in a half-full Home Depot bucket. Bucking and fighting on the soaked trap, getting no leverage, just sinking to the bottom and little air bubbles coming up. I was still showing a stunning lack of imagination about today's turn of events.

I closed the cupboard door. Thought a little harder, dug a little deeper. We'd already made up our minds to kill the thing as soon as we'd laid the trap. Now we were just being sadistic assholes. Besides, if my father-in-law had the guts to do the right thing, I did too.

"All right."

"Do I have to help you?" Jean asked plaintively.

"No. I got it." I couldn't stand to make her complicit in the act itself. I didn't look at her when I walked outside.

There was an orange bucket in the shed, covered in spiderwebs. On the inside, of course, there was mouse crap. I put on my leather work gloves. I took the bucket outside, stood over it, sighed, pulled the trigger on the nozzle attachment on the hose. It was on jet. The initial spray hit the bottom hard. It splashed my face and I startled. It misted onto my pants, spotting and darkening them. What a waste of water. But I wasn't about to half-ass this and not have a deep enough vessel. I would kill the mouse right this time. Fast. Merciful. I'd dump the bucket onto the plants when the deed was done. The lavender was struggling in the August heat—it would accept the rodenticide bath without judgment.

The fresh water roiled and bubbled as I filled the bucket and thought again of the mouse. In the kitchen, under the sink, the critter could have no idea he was closer than ever to death.

I went back inside. Bent down, took a knee, paused. In the cupboard, not much had changed. I reached a gloved hand in to grab the pad. That was when the little guy figured out it was going down. He craned his neck up at me. His tiny shoulders strained to raise his paws. Useless. They were so immersed in the mire they almost looked like part of the glue. The bit of the long tail that wasn't stuck flicked upward, then hit the pad and was trapped. He looked this way and that, down at four immobile feet—and now the furry chin was stuck. He vainly tried to raise his head, to see what was coming next. The pad didn't even lift off the cabinet. His pink dot of a nose quivered nonstop. A couple of his whiskers caught, but apparently not with enough surface area to hold. They flicked up again, leaving black marks on the trap.

He was completely immobilized, head supplicated at an awkward angle to the rest of his small body.

"Jesus Christ," I whispered, thick.

Outside, the mid-morning sun was clean and bright and still hot. It had rained for a minute overnight. The air was cotton in my nose. The bricks on the patio were a matte scarlet, contrasting with the shining orange bucket and the still, transparent water within. I held the trap and the waning life stuck to it, the light square pulled tight at the edges between my fingers. The nose and whiskers continued to vibrate. Mouse eyes are all black, no whites. You can't tell if they're widened in terror, but I felt they were. It must have been looking at me thinking, "Just get it over with, you bastard."

When I was young, very young, my family raised chickens. Rhodies, all of them. Rust-red, mild temperament, quick growers, good layers. A couple dozen every year. We'd slaughter them in the spring. I was too young to do the killing, but I'd round them up and bring them to my father. The memories are thirty years old, but they're the most recent I have of intentionally taking another life.

The translucent teardrop-shaped ears were plastered to the mouse's head, the only real sign it was scared out of its fucking mind. I stroked the body head to toe, told it that it was going to be all right, and that I was sorry. The ears didn't come up. I wasn't going to mouse-whisper the terror away. All the regret in the world wasn't going to change things now. I didn't cry or anything, but I was sorry. I don't believe in God and had no illusions there was a land of rainbows and unicorns waiting for the mouse when this was over.

I dropped it in. The rectangular pad sank to the bottom. Then it popped to the surface, mouse-side-up. Now it was soaked, fur clinging to the body, slick where it had once been fluffy, the miniscule frame outlined. Its sunken chest heaved.

"Oh God."

I reached in to flip the pad over, but I was clumsy and hasty. The index finger of my glove got well stuck to the pad. There was no way I'd be able to get it off without pulling it out of the water, and there was no way I was going to let the mouse get another gasp of air and then plunge it back under.

"Jesus Christ."

Resolved, I shoved it to the bottom. I stood there, elbow-deep in cold water, awkwardly bent over the bucket, and waited. I thought about wanting this to be over, or maybe never happening in the first place, and admired my own capacity for compassion while still finding a way to navigate the practical demands of the world.

I thought briefly about that Schrödinger physicist and how he thought up this situation where a cat was basically alive and dead at the same time. In my new state of compassionate competency, well—at this moment it seemed to me there was a pretty bright line between life and death.

I refused to look away. The mouse gradually stopped moving. It took probably only a few seconds, but you know how time is. How long should I wait now? I tried yet again to decide how to feel about this whole thing.

Of course, I found a way to forgive myself; it's not like the animal world is without its own brutalities.

My youthful menagerie had included cats and dogs—several of them because we didn't get them fixed. Most years we had puppies and kittens over the summers. I was home, so I was responsible for looking after them during the day. It was a joyous duty, mostly, except for this one summer. I was nine, maybe ten? We usually kept the kittens in the downstairs bathroom, in the bathtub until they were old enough to jump out. We left the door open so the mom cat could go in and out, though she rarely showed much interest.

I came home from the swimming pool one afternoon, dumped my bike in the dusty driveway, and excitedly went in to check on them. It was a mixed-breed crew of six. Black ones with white points, white ones with black spots, and a couple tabbies. I poked my head in and looked down into the white porcelain tub. The kittens were milling around, yowling, mewling. Some of them played together, tumbling over each other and batting their paws at the air.

At the far end of the tub lay one of the tabbies. Well, just the black and tan stripy body of a tabby. The kitten's head, about the size of a golf ball, lay not far from it. The bloody stump of the neck jutted from the body abruptly.

I backed out of the bathroom into the hallway. I came back in again. The head and the body still lay there. None of the other kittens even seemed to notice.

Staring at it, I began to feel panicked. Then guilty. Then ashamed. Seeing something that terrible made me shamefully sick. I didn't understand what had happened. Finally, I took my eyes off the decapitated kitten. I surveyed the rest, counting them, assessing. The other tabby was testing the slick walls of the tub. The fur around its mouth was dark and matted.

Dumbly, I looked back at the headless kitten. I glanced down the hallway, into the kitchen. Up the stairs. My parents couldn't know what happened. No one could. But the godawfulness of something like that had to stick somewhere. Someone had to take responsibility for it. It couldn't just *be*. So I took it, but I couldn't share it. I couldn't let anyone see it on me and make it real, even if it was in me now. Death. I'd never felt it that way before, inside me. The minute we're born death starts looking for a way in, and one way or another it finds it.

I took another step into the bathroom, and another. I got an old hand towel from the cupboard. When I reached in to pick up the body, the other kittens came right over. They mewed sweetly and licked my arm and swatted and tried to climb up and play. The one that had done it—that other tabby—it came over too. It looked at me, tilted its little head with its blue kitten eyes, and mewed. You couldn't see what was inside it. Wouldn't know that it had gnawed its brother's head off, except for that brick-red fur around its whiskers.

I don't remember how I felt about that kitten. I don't remember if I was mad at it, or sick by it. I don't remember, because I don't want to.

I brushed the other kittens off me gently. The limp fluffy body was cold when I took it away. The head was so light. The eyes were closed, that was good. Laid against the burnt-orange towel, pieces put back together, it just looked dead.

Rolled up, the bundle weighed nothing in my hands. I set it on the tiled bathroom counter. I don't think I looked in the mirror. Another glance at the kittens, all of them just sitting there looking up, eyes fixed on me. Even the cannibal tabby.

"What's next?" they seemed to ask in unison.

From the depths of my bedroom closet I retrieved an empty shoe box. I carried the towel-wrapped burden out of the bathroom and shut the door tight.

It was August. It was hot outside. I was still in my Muppets swimsuit when I dug the grave. I went deep, so other animals wouldn't dig it up. I don't remember what I told my parents when they got home that night and we were one kitten down. Certainly not the brutal truth. Not that their kid knew things now, knew death.

From far away, my cold fingers registered that the mouse hadn't moved for a very long time. The summer heat was picking up. My back hurt a little from the awkward angle over the bucket. In the hawthorn shrub next to me, the green leaves shining in the sun rustled. The thin branches gave a little sway. Birds nesting, or possibly mice running around. Animals going about their lives, hunting, sleeping, breeding. Maybe that little mouse family wondering why Dad wasn't home yet.

I yanked my hand out of the water and ripped the sticky pad and the small body from my glove. Dumped the thing in a plastic bag and threw it in the garbage can.

Watered the lavender and put the bucket back in the shed.

I sighed as I walked back toward the house. Relief came to me, finally. We'd get rid of those damn traps, all of them. We'd find another way, or we'd coexist. Suddenly the day seemed warm, not hot, and bright with possibility.

"Hey, hon?" I shucked my shoes in the mud room. "What do you say we go out for a while, take a ride?"

I was desperate to shake the morning off, and it was a lovely day for a drive. Turn the A/C all the way up and crank the windows down. Maybe we'd stop uptown and run into folks at the grocery store. We'd just gotten back from our first official retired snowbird stay down south, leaving reluctantly with promises to new friends to return soon. Here at home, though, there was still all the excitement to come of reconnecting with old friends: impromptu cookouts, wine and twilight on the deck and laughter. Deep purple and red sunsets that linger so long, you're shocked when night finally comes and it's time to say goodbye. You tell your guests to drive safe, then turn to your beautiful wife with a glimmer of hope that maybe it's not all over yet.

"Hon?"

I came through to the kitchen. Glanced at the cupboard under the sink. The dishwasher was droning away, *thunk, thunk, thunk.* I placed the palm of my hand on one of the rough-hewn beams holding up the old farmhouse. Leaned around into the living room.

"Jean?" I took a few more steps into the dining room.

There she was. Right there on the shining oak floor. Nothing at all wrong with her, except that her face was white and shiny and swollen, and her lips were blue, and instead of sitting on a chair she was lying on her side on the floor.

I rushed to her and fell to my knees, just like you'd see in a movie. We think we're better than clichés, but we're not. It hurt when I landed. It hurt so bad it gave me bruises and a headache, but that might have been from the shouting.

I stood, fell, and stood again. Staggered to the kitchen and riffled through the junk drawer for her EpiPen. I stabbed it into her thigh, plunged, started massaging her leg with both hands. Useless. I didn't know CPR, then. So I just shook her, and I shook her.

A small bee fell from inside her collar. There was a fat red welt on her neck, right below her ear where there used to be a gentle curve I'd just come to admire recently. She'd cut her graying hair short last month, because she'd always judged older women with long hair and wanted to get out front of that sin.

I stared at the tiny body on the floor next to Jean. Perhaps the bee had crawled into the house through the same little hole the mouse had. Either way, it lay there on the brightly polished dining room floor, dead. Just like Jean.

I lay down with my head right next to hers. I kissed her short, soft hair and tried to get a little closer to her, where she was now. Useless. For so long I'd stupidly thought of the end of life as a black-and-white proposition. Yet again, I had a brand-new perspective. Lying next to my wife, the two of us so still on the floor, I realized that physicist was right. You can be alive and dead at the same time.

———————————

Amy Drayer grew up a free-range kid on a charming island in the Pacific Northwest, then migrated south to attend Scripps College in California. She later moved to Washington, D.C., where she worked in politics and community organizing. Now living in Denver, Colorado with her wife, Amy is a graduate of the inimitable Lighthouse Writers Workshop Book Project and an active member of Rocky Mountain Fiction Writers and Sisters in Crime. Her debut mystery novel, Revelation, *is available anywhere books and e-books are sold. Learn more about Amy and all her work at MakahIslandMysteries.com.*

BREAD IN CAPTIVITY

by R.J. Rowley

Welcome, welcome to the Sanctuary of Rare Species!

Everyone, please come inside, into the viewing area. Thank you all for visiting today. Madam, you may take a seat here by the glass. Yes, that wall is high enough to keep you safe. And there's plenty of room for your kids. What are their names? Tommy and Sally, welcome. I can see you're excited—maybe a little rambunctious as well, but that's to be expected. This is a momentous occasion. How often do you get to see such a fantastical creature in captivity?

Oh, indeed, what you will see on the other side of this glass—in this perfectly recreated habitat—is the rare and wild *toastus levitas*, or flying toaster, if you will. It's taken us almost six months to catch our near-perfect specimen. Which wasn't easy, I can assure you. Though they can only fly up to roughly counter-height, they are slippery devils. And today, you—yes, you—will be the first members of the public to see this wondrous beast up close.

Now, before we release him into our terrarium
habitat so that you can gaze upon him, I'm afraid I must
go through a few rules.

One, please do not tap on the glass. That will spook
him. And we don't want to upset this little guy, do we?

Two, please do not throw anything into the terrarium.
That also will spook him.

Three, please do not take any flash photos. That will
set him off, too. Remember, he is a wild creature and not
yet fully adapted to this paradise we've made for him.

Finally, I know it will be tempting, but if he manages
to project an object—what we like to call a slice—over
the terrarium wall, please do not make a mad dash for it.
We have not yet determined if his crusty emissions are
poisonous.

What's that?

Why no, Tommy, *I* don't believe the toastus is
dangerous, but we're all going to do our best to respect
him, aren't we? Listen to your mother.

Yes, Sally, he is treated humanely. I promise... I
don't care what you saw on the news.

So, if you're ready to meet this great wonder of the
world, we will now... Release the Toaster!

Ah! You can see him over there beyond the
wheatgrass in the corner. He's slowly creeping out from
the entry tunnel. Now, what we've learned since catching
this specimen is that the toastus levitas is actually quite
shy. They hardly make any noise at all—outside of a
little metallic popping sound when they discharge—and
can become quite agitated when presented with shiny

objects like knives or forks. Why, this little guy even stung one of my colleagues, who approached him with a metal probe. The zap from that toastus just about turned the poor man's finger black.

Wait! I think something is happening.

Oh, you're in for a treat, ladies and gentlemen. Here he comes around the jelly patch, slowly making his way to the butter we left out for him. While the toastus levitas species does not consume melted butter—in fact, such oils would cause the toastus to secrete a most rancid musk—he does like to have such lubricants available when it comes time for him to release his daily slices, as sometimes they can be dry, hot, and uncomfortable to handle.

Yes, Sally, we do wear quilted mitts when we handle the slices. You're a smart little one, aren't you?

And yes, Tommy, I do believe we will get to see a slice ejection today. This little guy hasn't released a single slice since yesterday, and if he doesn't expel regularly, the hunks can be dark, hard, and sometimes charcoal-like in texture. Very unpleasant.

Now, since he seems a little hesitant about coming out from behind the butter trough, my colleague Brad is going to nudge him with a spatula—No, Brad! Not the metal spat—Oh, dear. Well, now you can say you've seen the electric sting of a toastus levitas in action. Quite painful-looking, isn't it?

Don't worry, everyone. Brad will be fine. He's going to pop off to the medical tent for a while to tend to that booboo.

No, Sally, I don't think the toastus is angry. He's just a little startled. Haha!

Meanwhile, look at our toastus levitas go. That little energy surge has got him up and darting about now. Quite, um, exuberant, isn't he?

Look at his silvery wings in full spread. Oh, he's up and swirling about left and right. This one is a very special specimen. Apparently, he can fly slightly higher than other toastus leviti our scientists have observed in the wild. We believe that is because we provide him with outlets to feed on when he's not in the terrarium. Those little jolts seem to have given him some extra oomph in his launch! But don't worry, he never makes it past the terrarium glass.

No, Tommy, it's not because he's fat. He's just not built for great flight.

What's that? I believe the gentleman in the back has a question.

Yes, sir, he is a full-sized adult. You can see by the six-inch span of his wings that he is a mature toastus. While in flight, he will keep his tail retracted into a compartment just south of his crumb disposal belly plate. You can see there the little nub of his plug peeking out at us.

Now, now, ladies. There is no need to fan yourselves or faint. Even the females have a plug. Which brings up a question I get asked all the time: How do you tell the gender of a toastus levitas? You know, is it a boy or a girl? Haha! Well, that's simple. The males tend to be smaller and have only two slots on their backs. Females are much larger, sometimes hosting as many as four slots on their backs. That's why their flight is often most inhibited—

Oh, gosh, sorry there, folks. Looks like our toastus got off course there and, uh, bumped the glass a smidge. I assure you though, he's just fine.

Madam, please, no flash photography. Selfies included. Do you see how the bright light makes him fly around all erratic? Let's allow him to calm down a bit, because...

Oh, oh! What's he doing now? Cover your eyes, children, he's about to release his crumb buildup—Ah, there he goes! The belly plate has opened, and he has expressed his crumbs onto the terrarium floor. So sorry you had to see that, folks. We usually try to clean that up before you get here.

No, Sally. I know your teacher told you that was a sign of duress, but I assure you it's perfectly normal. He's done that every day since he's been here. In fact, I'll bet if he's reached this stage of self-preening that means we're one step closer to what you all came to see today. The moment we like to call the "pop up."

Yes, I find it funny too, kids.

Well, our little toastus levitas has now settled back down and is nestling in the wheat. Isn't he precious when he's all peaceful and dark?

No, Sally, I don't think he looks shifty. He's meditating. Where's your mother?

As I'm sure you can imagine, we can interpret the mood of the toastus levitas by the coloring of those two slots on the back there. Do you see those, kids?

When those slots are dark, that means the toastus is calm and at rest. If they begin to develop a hint of color, say red or orange, then you'd better watch out, folks, because that means the toastus levitas is about ready to deliver.

Oh, wait a moment. Do you smell that?

Yep, take a deep whiff of that scent of rye…no, no, I think it's oat today, folks. That is the cologne of a toastus levitas in heat. Look! You can even see on the back that the slots are starting to change color.

Look closer, kids. Don't be shy. He can't come over the glass. See how his back slots have a red glow. Do you see that? What else do you see, ladies and gentlemen? You guessed it. There are two growths in the slot chambers. Do you notice them there?

So, everyone, keep your eyes on those back slots. Notice how the smell becomes stronger. Notice how that glow is downright orange. It's almost time. Get ready.

Here…he…goes!

Kaboom! Did you all see that?

The toastus levitas has popped his slices almost two feet in the air. That was quite a sight, wasn't it? I'm so glad you were here today to join us for this remarkable act of nature. It's really spectacular, don't you think?

Wait. What is your child doing? Tommy—is that Tommy? Hold on a second, Tommy, don't throw that muffin over the terrarium wall. The toastus levitas doesn't like muffins. They're too crumbly and will clog up his back slots and cause a most horrible burning sensation in his belly.

Dammit, Tommy—I mean, that's enough for now, son. Why don't you step away from the wall and take that seat next to your mother?

What was that, Madam? No, I can't bring that thing—I mean, our little friend—out so your kids can pet him.

Uh-uh, Tommy, don't hit the glass. You mustn't disturb the toastus further.

Madam, please come and get your son... Where's Sally?

Dear God. He's up again. He's taking flight! Holy breadcrumbs! Something's in there. What is it? I can't see.

Please, everyone, step back. We must move away from the terrarium. His crumb belly is full again, and you can see his back slots are red-hot.

Oh, no! Tommy! Sally! Get out of there. How did you get over—never mind. I'm coming. Wait. Oh, dear—

He's rammed it again. The glass...it's cracking. They told me it couldn't break. But it's cracking! He's coming through. Everyone, run! He's going to douse you with flaming crumbs. Run!

Oh, the humanity! Tommy's in the butter trough. Sally's hiding in the wheat. Why is he coming my way? Wait a minute, toastus. I've always been so kind to you. I've never fed you an oversized bagel, not even once. I didn't put the children in there. I only wanted to save them.

Why do you have your tail down and your plug out? Oh, dear mercy!

Why did the maintenance crew leave a tub of water in here? Someone, cover the outlet before he—too late! His prongs have attached. He's feeding on the electricity.

Do you see the murder in his eyes? Oh, toastus, I have not done this to you. I am not the one who put you in the cupboard! They are the ones. Those monsters who captured you. Not me. I'm just the visitors' guide. I'm a volunteer!

No, please don't come any closer. I beg of you. Don't knock me into the tub! Please, toastus, have mercy upon us all!

Zap!

——————————

R.J. Rowley is a joker of all trades who captures life's absurdities on the page and keeps them there until the proper authorities arrive. A Colorado native, she is the author of cozy-comedy memoirs, humorous fiction, and satirical guides to life. Outside of her library of books, other publications include satirical articles, short works of fiction, and random acts of poetry. For more information about past, present, and future publications, visit bexly.org or follow her (@bexlycomedy) on Facebook and Twitter.

THE RE-CREATION OF SAHMIK GHEE
by Paul Martz

I entered the Lake Lebarge outfitter's module with Sahmik Ghee's little finger in a bio carton.

Parka-clad traders waddled in behind me as I kicked snow off my boots. Like everyone, they bore the genetic mods for antarctic work—plump cheeks, big noses, and thick body hair. But some spoke into glasscells and had wires dangling from their ears. Lake Lebarge was less Alioth Three's southern frontier town and more a hub for corporate traders every day. The bars still served good Iapetian whiskey, though. And it was the closest place on the planet to reprint your partner.

A green line painted on the floor, barely visible under dirty puddles and scuff marks, led me past racks of provisions and sonic traps. I unzipped my parka. As I walked, two pendants around my thick neck swayed— one mine, one Sahm's.

The line stopped at the bioprinting desk. A badge over one breast identified the technician as Aliss Mae. She had the antarctic mods, but she was a desk jockey. She'd never touched the cold grips of a dog sled. I'd seen her before, though, and I knew she did good work.

I stated my business.

"Name of the reprint?" she asked, opening her glasscell.

"Sahmik Ghee, but I called him Sahm." I spelled it for her.

She paused for a moment and looked up at me. "I remember you. We printed Sahm just a few days ago, I think."

I nodded. "Right. But we had some trouble."

"Sorry to hear that." She turned back to her glasscell. "You got P.O.D.?"

Proof of death.

I placed the bio carton on her desk. Sahm's finger slept inside, packed in dry ice. A DNA test would confirm his identity, and forensics would prove he was dead when I snapped the icy little finger off his hand.

"Ready to give your statement?" She tapped controls on her glasscell to start a recording.

"The whole story?" I asked.

"From the beginning."

I met him in Plumtree. Horrible place for a market, Plumtree. Right on Alioth Three's equator and hot as blazes year-round. But for a snowshade hunter like me, it's the best place to meet exporters and peddle the fangs I harvest. It had been a tough market since corporate traders started undercutting my prices, and credit was tight. As I walked past the hagglers and the barkers boosting their pelts and off-world goods, I wondered if it might be my last visit to Plumtree.

I pitched my tent next to an importer dealing whiskey from the bogs of Iapetus. Setting up under the hot Alioth sun was a mite uncomfortable, modded for the antarctic as I was. I broke a sweat setting out my wares. As I cooled off in front of a fan, Sahm entered my tent.

He pressed his nose against the glass of my freezer unit like a kid at the off-world zoo, staring at the fangs on display. Exquisite trophies, them—a meter long, sharp as needles, and no melt or wear. They were still set in their crystal jaw, lined up like the teeth of a comb.

"Looks like ice, eh? But they're strong as steel, cut right through a man." I told him they were a crystal that formed only on Alioth Three, an arrangement of water molecules that defied analysis. Selling one set of fangs like that would keep me in business for a month.

"Let me show you my demok tusks," he said, forming a steamy oval on the cold glass with his breath. That's when I knew he was a trader—a hunter, like me. He had the tropical gene mods, with his dark skin and lean build.

Sahm's tan djellaba swayed as we made our way to his tent. He told me he hunted demoks on the Dry Plateau west of Plumtree. Corporate traders were putting the squeeze on him too, and he had to diversify to keep up profits. He showed me his handmade jewelry, polished fossils, and gemstones. Just trinkets, really. The demok tusks were his primary credit, and his were fine specimens. A real shame corporate traders had forced his price down.

Now the demok is no snowshade, but it's no tooth fairy either. You need guts to kill one. That's when I started thinking maybe Sahm and I could partner.

We met for beer later that evening. I figured corporate traders would ruin us both if we didn't team up, and I told him as much. By partnering in the antarctic, we could cut our overhead and share the profits.

He was open to partnering, but the cold worried him. He'd never seen snow except on the tops of distant mountains. As he fidgeted with his beer mug, he asked how he'd stay warm. A good question, that—given he'd never been out of the tropics. I told him about my heated habitation pod, the parkas, and the antarctic gene mods.

He looked me up and down, studying my girth and thick beard. "Okay. If I get those antarctic mods, I'll do it."

With that out of the way, we negotiated the terms. My offer was fair, but Sahm haggled over everything. "I'd get better pay for banja pelts," he said, and "Why are the taxes so high? You'll have to offset that." I thought he was driving a hard bargain, but the more I got to know him, the more I realized he was just a natural-born whiner. He even bellyached about the beer I bought him.

When it came time to talk reprints, I told him the truth. I needed as many as possible to make the partnership worthwhile. I warned him Alioth Three's antarctic has a hundred ways to kill a man. That's why we make backups. But reprinting only restores to the last backup; anything after that is gone.

As a demok hunter, he was no stranger to reprints. "You can't expect me to lose weeks of memories at that price," he complained. But after quite a back and forth, we finally agreed to one base reprint and three additional, with option to renew. That settled all the terms.

After we shook on it, Sahm pulled two neck-chains out of his djellaba, each with a shiny fossilized pendant seashell. He said they were some kind of symbiotic cephalopods that flourished on Alioth Three back when Earth was still a molten rock. He showed me how they fit together like two folded hands.

"It means we keep our word." And I saw in his eyes he was dead serious. He removed one chain and handed it to me, tucking the other back into his djellaba.

I'd never heard of that tradition. But I hung the pendant around my neck and told him I was a man of my word.

Once we'd completed our Plumtree business, we took the mag here, where I had my gear and puppet huskies in storage.

Now, Lake Lebarge is a southern frontier town, and the day we arrived was a cold one. Sahm was griping before we got indoors. That made sense; he was still modded for desert climes. So, the first thing we did was reprint him.

"You were on staff for that reprint," I said.

"I was. Give me a sec. Let me find those backups."
Aliss scrolled through data on her glasscell.

A creepy feeling, backups. All that nanotech
crawling inside your body, counting every cell,
molecule, and atom. Reducing you to numbers stored
and edited in a computer. But it's a necessity for the
antarctic trade.

"Oh yeah, here he is." She tapped her glasscell.
"Okay, continue."

When Sahm emerged from the printer, I hardly
recognized him. He was chubby like me, covered in thick
brown hair. He felt his dumpling cheeks and the blubber
around his waist. I'd been holding his shell pendant
while he was printed, so I placed it around his neck. It
barely fit.

"My neck's too big." He complained about
everything.

With my gear out of storage and the puppet huskies
roused from sleep mode, I paged a hoverbot to fly us
down to my base camp at the south territorial shelf. The
huskies leapt aboard, programmed to smell the hunt.
Soon we were pole-bound, flying south across
kilometers of frozen landscape.

We arrived in brisk weather, -83 degrees and a 20-
knot wind. Cold enough to freeze your eyes shut. The
puppet huskies loved it, though. They bounded into the
snow and in seconds were marking their territory.

My habitation pod was still anchored to the ice. While Sahm cleared the snow, I loaded the fuel and started the generator. Pale Alioth spends little time above the horizon, and it was dark before we finished booting the pod's environment. We set the hoverbot to return, fed the dogs, and watched the moons and stars dance heel and toe. But Sahm took no joy from the spectacle. The night was too cold for him, so we went into the pod to warm up.

"I didn't know it would be this cold," he said, rubbing his hands over the heat vent. "I don't think they gave me the right mods."

I chuckled. It took only a glance to see he had the right mods. He was fat as a pregnant demok, and his beard was thick as a banja pelt. How could he be cold? It made no sense. He kept griping. On and on he went, even worse than his whining in Plumtree.

When I thought I couldn't stand his raving any longer, he said to me, "If I die down here, promise me you'll cremate me. I don't want my body left in this unforgiving cold."

"Fine. Sure, I'll cremate you." I would've promised anything to get him to shut up. I didn't care that it made no sense. He knew what the contract said—three reprints. He knew he was coming back.

"You give me your word?" He lifted his pendant out of his parka and waited for my reply.

I'd forgotten about the pendants. I thought they were just for partnering, sealing our deal. But he was serious. I let out a breath as I retrieved the pendant from my shirt.

And with my pendant next to his, the two shells reflecting the pod's dim LEDs, I gave him my word.

Sahm took extra blankets when we sacked in, but he never warmed up. I listened to his teeth chatter all night, and he talked in his sleep. I covered my head with a pillow and slept as best I could.

We rose before sunrise. Sahm complained of the cold as soon as we started loading the sled with traps. "Is it always this gray and dismal here?" he asked. Nothing satisfied him. But the puppet huskies begged for the harness, and soon our sled was making route over the dark snow.

We entered a valley in the heart of my claim, deep in snowshade territory. Statues of snow and ice stand vigil there, carved by the howling wind. They're goblins, I say. You never see them move, but from one visit to the next they're never quite in the same place. We mushed past them as they brooded in dawn's first pale streaks.

We stopped in a lane among the goblins, a perfect spot to trap snowshade. Sahm said he was too cold to move. He crouched on the sled, arms crossed, rocking back and forth. He was useless. I would've been better off partnering with a banja hunter.

I was about to remind him of our contract when I heard the puppet huskies howling over the wind. An awful alarm, a pack of puppet huskies wavering out of tune like the pipes of Mizar. Why the programmers gave them such a ghastly sound, I'll never know.

But that alarm could mean only one thing.

And I hadn't prepared a trap. That made the sound all the more dreadful.

Have you ever seen a snowshade coming? A swirling vortex of snow. The crisp sound of ice growing into crystalline bones. Snowflakes joining into layers of muscle and tendon. Fully formed, it stood over us, an elemental of snow and ice as tall as the goblins. It exhaled a frozen wind from its open maw.

That's when I saw the precious fangs—our quarry, the whole reason for our expedition. They were perfect! Clear as cut gemstones, longer than I'd seen in years, and serrated like kitchen knives. The buyers in Plumtree would pay top credit for a museum-quality set like that, enough to keep my expeditions running for months. But how could I harvest them? The snowshade was already upon me. I'd be dead before I could set the trap.

With the puppet huskies howling and those fangs sparkling in the pale blue dawn, I'd all but forgotten about my useless partner. Sahm was still on the sled and hadn't moved a muscle since we left the pod. He stood to back away, but, stiff and awkward from the cold, he caught his boot on the sled and fell. The snowshade towered over him.

Now, I'm not the kind of trader who uses his partner for bait. I'd contracted with Sahm for only three reprints, and I didn't fancy using one the first day out. But I'm running a business here. If I didn't harvest those fangs, corporate traders surely would. Besides, once he fell, he was good as gone anyhow. There was really no choice.

And those fangs, they were incredible! Ask any trader, they'd have done the same.

I waded through the powdery snow to put Sahm between me and the snowshade, hoping to buy enough time to set the trap. Those controls are hard to set with thick gloves, and I fumbled a bit.

Sahm screamed. That made me drop the trap.

The creature held Sahm in its jaws.

Aliss drummed her fingers. "I don't understand. If Mr. Ghee was devoured, how did you obtain the P.O.D.?" She pointed at the carton.

"I'm getting to that."

Sahm was no tiny morsel, not with those antarctic mods, and blood formed red icicles as the snowshade devoured him. Now that was a scare, 'cause maybe eating my partner damaged the fangs. But I could see they were intact, still sharp and unbroken. I exhaled in relief, my breath a frosty mist.

I dug the sonic trap out of the snow while the creature struggled to get Sahm down its gullet. When the puppet huskies yipped, I knew the beast had finished its meal. It crouched and eyed me.

Arming the trap left me little time to flee before it pounced. My bones rattled as the trap sent out its sonic waves. The snowshade shook apart, and I fell, struck by chunks of ice and snow that had been muscle and bone only a moment before. A close escape, I tell you, by the hair of my brow.

I stood and brushed myself off. The puppet huskies paraded nervously, sniffing with their sensors where the snowshade once stood. Only a pile of snow and ice was left.

In the debris, a glitter caught my eye. I made straight for it, ignoring Sahm's foot sticking out of the icy rubble. There it was, a full set of fangs sparkling in the weak antarctic light. I carried the crystal jaw to the sled, careful to not cut myself on the serrations. The pointed cusps were dazzling, as sharp as needles. I imagined the bids this trophy would bring at auction. What luck, to harvest this our first day out!

Sahm? Oh, he'd been flash-frozen in the snowshade's icy stomach. One of the huskies latched onto his boot and dragged his corpse out of the rubble. His lips and eyelids were pulled back, frozen in a grotesque grinning mask. God! I couldn't stand the sight of the thing. I turned away, took out my flask, and pulled a shot of Iapetian whiskey.

Now, I had a mind to teach Sahm a lesson and leave him right there. He'd been a useless partner, and I'd had enough of his sniveling about the cold. Why bother cremating him? He wouldn't remember a thing since his last backup. Wouldn't even remember asking to be cremated. I took another sip and cursed him under my breath.

Two puppet huskies played tug of war in the snow, fighting over a glove they'd pulled from Sahm's corpse.

Behind them sat the sled with those glimmering fangs—immaculate, brilliant, priceless. Sahm had helped me take that harvest, in his own miserable way. I couldn't deny him his last request, and I didn't need to see that pendant frozen to the fur of his parka to know it. I would cremate him. It was the least I could do.

I knew a spot on my claim where the wind had cleared the snow and exposed coal seam. That was where I'd make good on my promise. Sahm hadn't frozen in a cargo-friendly position, but I wrestled the corpse onto the sled and made do with one stiff leg sticking out to the side. With the fangs secured, I mushed the dogs. We made the bare patch by sunset.

An open fire won't consume a body by itself. Not hot enough, especially not in the antarctic. You've got to have an enclosure, like a furnace. I found a small cave in a rocky outcropping and pushed the corpse to the back.

That's when I remembered I needed proof of death. So I crawled into the dark hole and snapped off that little finger. I took Sahm's pendant, too. His corpse stared back at me with icy, unblinking eyes. I knew the next time I saw those eyes, I could tell him I'd kept my word.

I piled in raw coal until the cave was packed full, soaked it with ethanol, and lit it.

I took the sled back a ways to keep from melting those fangs. Didn't fancy smelling Sahm cook, either. But the puppet huskies smelled him with their sensors, and they howled as the greasy smoke turned the twilight black as ink.

Aliss sat back and let out a breath. "Well, the genetic mods we gave him were standard antarctic thermal mods. That's good enough most of the time, but some people still report feeling abnormally cold, like your partner. We could amplify the thermal mods for an extra layer of fat. You want us to add that?"

Now, that was an idea. As soon as Sahm came out of the printer, he and I would head south for another expedition. And new memories weren't part of the backup, so as far as he was concerned it would be his first all over again. That meant I'd have to listen to him groan about the cold. If Aliss could boost his thermal mods and make him a bit warmer, maybe he wouldn't complain so much. Maybe I could get a good night's rest in the pod.

But…our previous expedition had worked quite well. I'd already received a credit advance for those fangs from my exporter. For that kind of bounty, maybe I could tolerate a little complaining. Maybe having Sahm immobilized from cold made him the perfect partner.

"No thanks," I answered. "Just use the standard mods, same as before."

Of course I'd tell Sahm what happened. There's no way to hide reprinting. One glance at a calendar and he'd know he lost a couple of days. I'd pay him his share of the profits, too, just like we agreed. We had a contract. I'm a man of my word.

Aliss paged me after a couple hours, and she brought Sahm out of the printer lab, just like new.

He felt his hairy dumpling cheeks and the blubber around his waist. Too bad it wouldn't be enough to keep him warm. I took his pendant from around my neck and handed it to him.

"My neck's too big," he said.

He was making this too easy.

When Paul Martz read "The Cremation of Sam McGee" in a collection of classic poetry, he knew it had to be retold as science fiction—and he was the only retired computer programmer and former punk rock drummer who could tell it.

An RMFW member since 2018, Paul writes kick-butt speculative fiction short stories and blogs about accessible technology. His upcoming novel will be available as soon as he writes and publishes it. You can cyberstalk him at paulmartz.com.

WHO WE WERE THEN
by John Mummert

It was dark by the time we rolled into Dyersburg. We scarfed down cheeseburgers and fries at the Dairy Queen—Darrell also inhaling two chili dogs—and continued south toward the Middle Forked Deer River. Four of us were stuffed into the cab of Scott's 1970 white-over-blue Ford Ranger, a camper shell over the bed and his little johnboat on the trailer bouncing along behind us. I had the spot by the door. Darrell was next to me, stuck in the middle because he was short enough to get his knees in front of the eight-track pounding out REO Speedwagon while we kept time on the cracked dashboard. Marie shared the driver's seat with Scott, who entertained us with assorted lewd verses of *Barnacle Bill the Sailor* during lulls in the tape. Marie shook her head and every so often gave him a disapproving look. Give her a few beers, and she'd admit to knowing most of the words herself.

We were three months from graduation. Darrell was four months from Navy boot camp. I was six months from college in St. Louis. Scott and Marie would be married in less than a year. He hadn't asked her yet, but we took it as a given.

Whenever Scott drew a breath, we talked about the week ahead, about our plans after graduation. Our basketball team getting screwed in the regionals. A classmate busted with a duffle bag full of Thai sticks. Our hopes for how much shorter the dishcloths Janet Covington passed off as skirts might get.

"Pervs," Marie said. "Best not be hearing any talk about *my* skirts."

Janet was on our minds because Scott and I had run into her at Peterson's that afternoon while discussing what kind of chips we wanted and how many eggs we needed. We looked up to see her standing in the aisle. There Scott and I were. Shopping. Like we were married or something.

Janet smiled. I was immediately stricken with the inability to speak.

"Bet this looks pretty funny, don't it?" Scott was never plagued with the inability to speak. His quick tongue, and I suppose his curled brown hair and slender build, gave him an edge with girls, though not as much as he seemed to believe.

Janet pushed back her long blond waves. "Well, I wasn't going to say anything."

"We're going on a fishing trip. You oughta come with us."

"Mmm. Sounds like fun."

I was well on my way to believing she might come.

"We'll make room. We'll leave Darrell at home." Scott would have offered to leave me at home if I hadn't been standing there. I'd have offered to leave Scott if I'd been able to speak.

"Well, I have plans. Hope you have fun." Janet smiled again and walked away, probably rolling her eyes and thinking *Oh sure, like I'm going camping with you goobers.*

"Boy, I'd like to take her along," Scott mumbled after we watched her stroll out of sight, her legs and the sway of her hips no longer an immediate distraction. Big talk on his part, seeing as Marie was going with us.

"I'll say," I replied in my usual idiot fashion.

We finished picking out our food, then stopped at the Liquor Barrel for a couple cases of Little Kings. Scott's recent birthday made both of us eighteen—the legal age in those days—so we no longer had to worry about which clerk was working. We picked up Marie, headed out to the edge of town to get Darrell, and managed to get away before his liquored-up dad could get home and start giving us hell about whatever he was pissed off about that day. I know it embarrassed Darrell when his old man started in on him in front of us. *Darrell—turn that goddamn music down! Damn it, Darrell—you boys know what time it is?* Scott had persuaded his parents to let Darrell stay at their house a few times when Darrell's dad was on a major bender. I think Darrell joined the Navy to get out of the house.

It was well after eleven o'clock when we reached the campsite. Scott had to hunt for the entrance road, a crater-filled dirt path that stretched the definition of road beyond reason. We passed an old Quonset hut a couple miles off the blacktop. About three miles beyond the Quonset, a dilapidated Shasta travel trailer sat deeper in the woods. No one was around. Fifty yards beyond the Shasta, we parked near the slough-like shore of a small oxbow lake, next to a fire pit surrounded by a ring of large stones.

Thick woods encircled oxbows and sloughs in the Middle Forked Deer floodplain stretching west toward the Mississippi. Scott knew about the site because his uncle worked for the timber company that had owned the twenty-five thousand acres of surrounding land before turning it over to the state. Scott swore it was just the place to spend our last spring break, a change of scenery from our usual campsite along the Saline. So we'd driven nearly two hundred miles south, darn near to Memphis.

Not one of us would ever make a worse decision.

We sat under the starlight drinking Little Kings. Darrell fired up a joint, which set Scott off. Scott was far from a prude, but for some reason he wanted nothing to do with pot.

"Damn, Red, I've told you—"

A stare from Darrell cut him off. Scott occasionally tried to attach that nickname because of the red flattop on Darrell's head. Darrell wouldn't have it. He was easy-going, but he hadn't made all-conference linebacker at his small size by being easily bulldozed.

Marie had already claimed the front seat of the truck. She wasn't about to sleep in back with us guys, and she wasn't about to mess around with Scott while Darrell and I were near. So the three of us unrolled our sleeping bags in the truck bed, under the camper shell. Darrell and I thought Scott deserved to be stuck back there with us since he'd started all the talk that got us fantasizing about Janet and her microscopic skirts. The arrangement later went south on me as well, when Darrell's chili dogs started making themselves known.

"Dang," Scott said. "I think a possum done crawled up in here and died."

We got up the next morning, our clothes looking as if we'd slept in them—we had—and our hair all askew. Except for Marie, whose thick black hair was mussed in that   I-just-woke-up-next-to-you-and-I-want-to-do-it-again way. Seeing her with that look, I was glad she'd slept in the front seat.

I liked Marie. I didn't have trouble talking to her like I did Janet and most other girls in school. Most other girls on the planet. I suppose Marie being unavailable made it easier. I'd never had the nerve to talk to her before she and Scott started dating.

We built a fire, made a pot of coffee, and attacked a pile of scrambled eggs and bacon. Scott chased Marie with a handful of ice until she gave him a glare suggesting he think hard about all the places his hands wouldn't be roaming in the near future if he dumped ice on her. We launched the boat into the adjacent oxbow, set and baited a trot line, and spent the rest of the morning fishing with no luck other than a big catfish Marie caught.

"You guys best watch when I get invited to be on *American Sportsman*," she crowed.

We ran the trot line late in the day. It too looked a bust, two measly crappies, until I hauled in a large paddlefish snagged on one of the hooks. "Got some good eating now," Darrell said.

As twilight approached, Darrell rekindled the fire and Marie prepared potatoes for frying. Scott and I had finished cleaning the fish when a dog came out of the woods. It was an average-sized mutt, its black fur streaked with mud and matted with burs. It growled, a bark here and there, a cascade of drool spilling from its mouth.

"Sucker looks mean," Scott said. "No collar."

Darrell retreated to the opposite side of the fire. "Bet it doesn't belong to anyone, being way out here."

"Easy, fella," I said to the dog.

"Well, I'm sure not planning to get bit." Scott eased his way to the truck, reached into his pack, and brought out a pistol and a box of ammunition.

"What are you doing?" Marie asked.

"Bet that mongrel's never had a rabies shot," Scott said.

"You're gonna shoot it?" Marie's voice was disapproving, but she was moving to the opposite side of the truck as she spoke.

"It's probably afraid of us," I said. "It's not coming any closer." I didn't believe Scott actually intended to shoot the dog. He could be insensitive, but I'd never known him to be consciously cruel.

"Even if it doesn't bite, it's liable to howl all night and keep us awake." Scott slipped bullets into the cylinder while watching the dog.

I grew uneasy about his intentions. "Throw some bacon out in the woods. Give it something to chase after."

"It'll keep hanging around hoping to get fed."

"So fire in the air and scare it off. It could belong to somebody. What if they show up looking for it?" My belief that Scott wouldn't shoot the dog was draining away.

"Always possible, Great White Dog Hunter," Darrell said.

"We're the only ones here," Scott said. "That trailer and that Quonset we passed don't get used except as weekend hunting and fishing camps. Mutt's a stray got dumped out here."

"Well, don't miss and make him mad," Darrell said. "He'll bite one of us for sure."

I hoped that would change Scott's mind, but as the dog continued growling and glaring at us, part of me wondered if there wasn't a choice. But it bothered me, and I should have done something more, tried harder to calm the dog. I had a dog at home. I was pretty good with them. But that meant standing up to Scott. He was impulsive; it wasn't easy to apply the brakes once he got an idea in his head. Darrell could do it, but I never had the backbone. We'd been friends a long time. Scott ran the show. I was always the sidekick.

Scott took a step toward the dog, aimed, and fired.

I don't know what I expected. That the dog would fall over like on TV? Instead, it whirled as the bullet ripped a bloody gash into its haunch. Its growl turned into a squeal of pain and fear I felt tearing into my own flesh. The dog lunged, dragging a rear leg, snarling its desire to take a chunk out of any of us it could reach. Marie jumped onto the hood of the truck as the rest of us backpedaled several yards.

Darrell peeked from behind a black gum tree, wielding a fallen limb like a club. "Nice shooting, Marshal Dillon."

Scott grinned without taking his eyes off the dog. "Bite me." He took three slow steps closer. The dog was wailing, trying to reach the wound in its thigh. Scott aimed, fired again.

The shot hit the dog square between the eyes. It went silent except for a final involuntary whimper and a thump as it hit the ground.

"Shit," Marie gasped. "Did you have to make it suffer first?"

"I didn't mean that to happen," Scott said. "It turned sideways as I fired."

Scott hunted often, and I believe he intended a clean shot. I doubt the effort meant much to the dog.

We found a piece of rusty corrugated tin and rolled the bloodied dog onto it. It was innocent now, smaller than it first appeared, any air of menace gone. Clean it up, put a collar on, and someone might have had a nice pet.

The dog's squeal of pain rang in my ears. My irritation gnawed at me—I knew I could have stopped this.

We dragged the dog into the woods, quite a ways we figured, and buried it under a pile of brush. We should have gone deeper into the woods. And we should have buried it for real.

We awoke late the next morning and took our time fixing breakfast. I hadn't slept well. It was colder. The fog lifted by the time we finished eating, and we saw an old junker of a Dodge pickup with a full camper on the back parked behind the Shasta. Someone had come in during the night.

We spent the rest of the morning fishing along the shore. We heard shooting deep in the woods in the early afternoon, but saw no one until a large johnboat crawled out of the overhanging branches at the south end of the oxbow. It was riding low, as if it might be taking on water. As the boat drew closer, we saw it was loaded down with buckets of fish and piles of ducks and turtles. A bag seine and a landing net rested across the bow. There were two men in the boat, dressed in coveralls, hip waders, and insulated hunting jackets. Both held shotguns. The heavyset fellow near the front nodded to us and raised a finger in acknowledgment. The lankier man at the rear stared at us, pausing only to spit a stream of tobacco juice over the outboard. They disappeared around a bend at the north end of the oxbow, and we heard the motor switch off.

"Those boys are poaching," Scott said. "Some of these fellows out here do a little. Never seen anybody with that big a load. Might be using a fish telephone."

"Or a bunch of M-80s," Darrell said. "And I don't imagine that seine's legal."

"Must be their truck come in last night," Marie said.

"I reckon," Scott said. "I don't aim to go snooping around. This isn't like ole Randy Witherspoon back home, shooting a deer out of season now and again. These boys are big-time. No telling what else they're into."

"Bet they didn't expect anybody to be out here," Darrell said.

"Don't imagine they'll pay us any mind so long as we keep to our business," Scott said.

The poachers made numerous trips carrying their haul from their boat to the camper on their Dodge. Later we heard them shouting, yelling into the woods. They continued calling as they wandered in our direction, shotguns over their shoulders.

"Beau! Beau!"

"How you fellows doing?" Scott asked when the poachers reached us.

"Doing real good." The lanky one eyed our camp and everything in it before settling his stare on Marie. "How's the fishing?"

"Not bad," Scott said. "Looking for somebody?"

"My mangy, no-good dog. Sumbitch knows to come when I call. I'll beat his ass good."

It made sense they had a retriever or a coonhound with them. My heart lurched nonetheless.

"Aw, Mason, don't git all tore up," the heavyset fellow said. "Reckon he's around here somewheres trying to rustle up something to eat. Come on, let's finish our business and git so's we can find a store. I need me an RC."

Mason glared at him. "Be finished when I say, Donnie. I ain't the one forgot your cola."

Donnie pursed his lips. His face took on a stony appearance.

"Dog get away from you?" Darrell asked.

Mason gestured toward the Shasta. "He stays out here, keeps watch of my camp so nobody does no snooping."

I caught Scott's eye for a fraction of a second. The dog did belong to someone, and they did come looking for it. Darrell drew a slow breath and held it. Marie bit her lip. We all knew.

Mason grinned through several days of beard growth. He wasn't being friendly. "Y'all seen any game wardens out here?"

"No, we haven't seen anybody since we got here," Scott said.

"Good." Mason leered at Marie. "That's real good."

The poachers continued to the slough, then south along the oxbow, calling for the dog.

Scott blew out a breath. "That mangy-ass dog was theirs? Hope we hid it good."

I stared at the ground, then looked up in exasperation. "If they find it…" *Damn it, I told you it might belong to someone*, I wanted to say. *If you'd done something when you should have*, I told myself.

"Maybe we oughta get out of here," Darrell said. "I got a bad feeling about those guys. Reckon they're not too crazy about us being here."

"Creeps," Marie muttered. She hadn't flinched while Mason was staring at her, but now she hugged her arms around herself. Unease filled my gut.

"Listen," Scott said. "We haven't seen any dog."

Shotgun blasts erupted from the direction the poachers had gone. We decided to load our gear and get Scott's boat out of the water so we wouldn't have to mess with it in the morning, when we planned to head home. Leaving sooner might have been on all our minds. Scott backed the truck nearer the water, and we hoisted the boat onto its trailer.

We'd pulled the trailer forward and finished tying the boat down when the poachers returned. Each cradled his shotgun with one arm, the other hand wrapped around the feet of a bunch of ducks. None of us were about to mention ducks weren't in season. They walked along the edge of the slough toward their own boat. Donnie looked at his watch and pointed toward the Shasta. They were arguing about the need to get on the road with their poaching haul.

"Let's put these here away first," Mason finally said, "then stash the boat."

They left the path to cut through the woods to the Shasta. A shortcut. One that might take them near the brush pile covering the dog. My heart accelerated.

"Sure hope you guys buried it good," Marie mumbled as we lost sight of the men among the hardwoods and brush.

The poachers were out of sight longer than it should have taken them to reach the Shasta.

Mason broke the silence. "Tarnation and hellfire!"

"Here they come," Darrell muttered.

Mason marched toward us, clearly pissed and getting more so as he approached. He had dropped his ducks. Donnie waddled alongside, trying to keep up.

"Don't let it git up your britches, Mason," Donnie said. "Ain't worth it. Gotta get this load down to Memphis pronto. Good money riding on this."

Mason ignored him. He stopped and spit a stream of tobacco juice into our fire pit. His eyes widened and slid from one of us to another in succession. He cradled his shotgun like a baby.

"Which one of you shot poor Beauregard?"

"Mason," Donnie said, "we ain't got the time. We don't know for sure they done it."

"Beauregard? That your dog?" There was a tremor in Scott's voice. His prodigious BS skills might not be enough this time.

Mason squinted at Scott, spit his wad of tobacco onto the ground between them. "You know it's my dog. And you said you ain't seen nobody else out here. So who was it shot poor Beau, finest dog ever lived?"

"Mason." Sweat beaded on Donnie's chin. "Jeez. We can find us another watchdog. Hell, Beau's just a stray we found out here anyways."

"Shut the hell up, Donnie. You ain't in charge here." Mason hadn't taken his eyes off Scott. "You the one shot Beau?" Then he turned to Marie. "Or was it this pretty lady? How about it, honey? You shoot my faithful ole hound dog? Got me an idea or two how you can make it up to his poor, grieving master."

Marie shook her head, looked away. I'd once seen her bloody an older boy's nose after he slammed his girlfriend against the gymnasium wall. Mason wouldn't scuttle away licking his wounds the way that kid had.

"Okay," Scott said, "I shot your dog. He was acting mad. I couldn't risk—"

"You lying little shit!" Mason gestured at the Illinois license plate on Scott's truck. "Y'all ain't from around these parts. Your mommy know where to come looking if you wasn't to come home?"

"For chrissakes, Mason," Donnie hissed.

It dawned on me Mason was right; no one knew exactly where we were. It wouldn't be hard to hide a body in these woods so it'd never be found. It would have been nice if we'd taken advantage of that when we were trying to hide the dog.

Darrell stood across the fire pit from Scott and Mason. He cleared his throat, caught Donnie's attention.

"Look, there ought to be a reasonable way to make this right."

Donnie took a cautious step forward. "Well, could be—"

"Stay right there, Donnie." Mason ran a hand along the barrel of his shotgun, a caressing gesture. "I'll decide how this'll be made right."

"Mason, you'll screw up a real good deal we got here."

I was standing at the front of Scott's boat, next to his truck's lowered tailgate, on the opposite side from everyone else. My heart was racing. I looked around, hoping someone—another fishing party, a game warden, Boy Scouts, anyone—would show up, provide a distraction so we could get the hell out of there. Marie stood at the other end of the tailgate, on the other side of the boat trailer and hitch. She glared at Mason, but her arms trembled. Scott licked his lips, looked sick to his stomach.

Mason moved his finger onto the trigger guard of his shotgun. "So, what you think a fella oughta do here, kid?"

The thought we should run, hide until the poachers were gone, flashed in my mind. Hike fifty miles to Dyersburg. Ridiculous, I knew. I was the only one with anywhere to run, shielded by Scott's truck and boat, with dense woods behind me. But I knew I couldn't even if my legs had been capable. Scott had been a dumbass—a special talent of his—about the dog, but we'd been friends a long time. Would I really run away and let someone shoot him? Or Darrell? Marie? Everyone I knew, everyone Marie, Scott, and Darrell knew, would learn what I'd done, the humiliation beyond my comprehension, my self-respect unsalvageable.

I'd never imagined dying might be better than anything until that moment.

My eyes continued darting about until they landed on the truck bed. Scott's pistol, which he hadn't returned to his pack, lay there. I'd fired it a few times, shooting at bottles and tin cans with Scott and Darrell. I was anything but proficient. Scott generally didn't keep his guns loaded. Leaving one out was unusual. Those things didn't occur to me as I slid the pistol from its holster.

I'd taken a couple timid steps toward the rear of the boat when I heard a soft thump, something hitting the ground. The pistol had slipped from my shaking hands. My fumbling movements drew a brief glance from Donnie, but he was preoccupied with Mason. No one else paid any attention to me. I grasped the boat to steady my nerves, leaned over in as smooth a motion as I could manage, felt for the pistol. I picked it up, held on tight, and continued sliding along the boat. Shivers passed through me, and the pistol barrel tapped against my leg. I couldn't swallow.

Scott put his hands on his knees, his breathing heavy. "Look, this—this here's just between you and me. Nobody else hurt your dog. Just…me."

Whatever Scott's faults, he would never have considered running and leaving the rest of us behind.

"You asking for mercy from this here court?"

Donnie threw an arm in the air. "Oh, criminy, Mason."

"Come on," Darrell urged Donnie. "You're not gonna let him do this, are you?"

Mason was less than fifteen feet away. I thought to raise the pistol, order him to drop his shotgun. But I knew it would come out of my mouth as no more than a squeak. Worse than trying to talk to Janet Covington. Mason might rupture his spleen laughing at me.

Or I could shoot Mason, and he'd fall over with a shoulder wound and surrender. As if I could shoot that well. As if this was *Gunsmoke*. I'd seen what that pistol did to Mason's dog, the blood-soaked gash in its haunch, its shattered head. I didn't hunt. I couldn't have shot a deer or a squirrel. What made me imagine I could shoot another person?

Mason winked at Marie. "I got plans for us, darling."

The assumption that my empathy for a deer would shift to Mason vanished in that moment.

Mason leveled the shotgun, his finger on the trigger, and pointed it at Scott. I leaned into the side of the boat, clenched the pistol with both hands, rested my wrists and forearms on a tackle box. If Mason hadn't been arguing with Donnie and threatening Scott and leering at Marie, he'd have noticed me sooner. Now he caught movement out of the corner of his eye and turned toward me, sneering, the shotgun still pointed at Scott. Adrenaline, maybe panic, surged in me.

I pulled the trigger; I don't know how many times. There were four bullets left—those Scott hadn't needed for the dog.

Scott dropped to the ground, perhaps expecting the pain of a gunshot. Marie screamed his name. Donnie hit the ground and covered his head.

Mason staggered sideways, staring right at me. The sneer on his face turned to shock as the shotgun slipped from his hands. A pulsing red ooze in the center of his chest mixed with the grime on his coveralls. He fell with a pronounced thud. A crack sounded as his head struck a stone around the fire pit.

I leaned harder into the boat to keep from collapsing. Scott crawled to Marie, who was close to hysterical. Darrell was nowhere to be seen, until his red flattop poked from behind an oak where he'd taken cover.

"Crap," Darrell said as he scanned the camp. "Holy mother bucket of crap." He gazed at me, held up both hands.

"Easy, kid. Take it easy." Donnie was on one knee, his hands out and away from his body, his shotgun on the ground. He nudged Mason, then kicked him to be certain. "Reckon Mason won't shoot nobody today. Tomorrow neither. What say you lower that pistol so it doesn't go off and hit one of us innocent bystanders? Don't worry. My gun's on the ground. Ain't even loaded. Let's all take us a deep breath and think our way through this here mess."

Darrell stepped over to where Mason lay. He opened Mason's shotgun as if to unload it, then frowned and set it aside. He looked at me until he'd drawn my attention, then held up a hand as he moved around the rear of the boat to where I stood slumped against the side, still clutching the pistol.

"There wasn't any choice," he murmured. He pulled the pistol from my hands—the last time my hands would ever touch a gun—and laid it in the bottom of the boat. "Even Kenny would say there wasn't any choice," he said, referring to a cop we knew back home.

Donnie stood and regarded each of us in turn. "Well, now. Appears we got ourselves a bit of a predicament."

"Suppose we gotta get the sheriff?" Scott said. He and Marie were huddled beneath the truck's tailgate. His eyes had a glazed, faraway look. A look of being lost.

Donnie laughed and clapped his hands together. "Good one, kid! You think I want a lawman out here asking questions? Got me a sweet deal here. Me and Mason and a couple other fellas, we hunt and fish these parts regular. Maybe not according to the law. You follow? Got us some regular buyers—folks willing to buy anything a fella can shoot, trap, or catch. Ain't looking to have business ruined 'cause Mason's got a temper."

It wasn't the reaction any of us expected.

"So." Darrell flexed his jaw. "What are you planning to do?"

"Well, old Mason here—may his sorry-ass excuse for a soul rest in peace—he was big dog in these parts." Donnie chuckled. "Big dog. Kinda funny, ain't it? Well, there's gonna be a new boss of this operation now. Lots nicer fellow. And Mason disappearing oughta make any peckerwood wanting to horn in on this territory think long and hard about what might've happened to him. If you catch my drift."

We caught his drift. I'd made Donnie the big dog and furnished him with a hardened reputation.

"Seems like somebody might be looking for him," Darrell said.

Donnie scratched his chin. "Nah. He's got a wife, but her and the kids done moved out on account he beats the hell out of her. He's got most other folks scared of him, too. Not many gonna miss him."

"Just gonna leave him here?" Darrell said.

"Why, that'd be downright uncivilized. Got a couple shovels up at the trailer. Gonna need you fellows to help bury the ole boy so I can get on down to Memphis. Got a buyer waiting on us. Waiting on me, I oughta say."

Donnie and Darrell dragged Mason into the woods. Scott followed, carrying the shovels. Marie stayed behind with me.

"You okay?" she asked as we sat on the tailgate. "He might have killed us. Might all be dead. He might have…" She shuddered and locked her arm through mine.

"He had to shoot that goddamn dog," I said in a whisper. I jumped up and raced behind a hickory, where I fought the desire to puke. Fought the desire to fall apart. A panicky check for blood on my clothes. I was in a fog. Marie brought a canteen of water, hugged me. She never told anyone the state I was in.

It took forever for them to bury Mason. Every time a shovel hit the ground, I felt it go through my skull and down my spine. They made sure it would be far harder to find Mason than it had been to find his dog.

"It'd be best if y'all got on out of here and didn't come back around these parts," Donnie said when they returned. He didn't need to say it twice.

"All this to shoot a dog," I said as we watched Donnie make his way back to the Dodge. I was shivering, but not from the cold.

Scott started to turn my way. "It might've bit—"

"It wasn't going to bite anyone," I snapped.

Scott looked away. "I didn't…"

"Damn it," I gasped and walked away to wait by the truck.

"I screwed this up bad, didn't I?" Scott mumbled to Marie before they got in the truck. Marie's response was sharp in tone, but I couldn't make out her words.

I recall little of the drive home, aside from Darrell's emphatic finger in my chest at a gas station in Union City. "Not your fault."

Everyone was quiet in the truck, no more than occasional stilted conversation in which I took no part. The eight-track remained silent. I stared out the window, avoided Scott's eyes and he mine.

Images spun through my mind the rest of the night and long after. The bloody dog. The bubbling red grime on Mason's chest. Visions of a sheriff pulling us over, taking me away. The sound of shovels splitting the ground.

And the frown on Darrell's face when he opened Mason's shotgun. Was the gun not loaded? Had Mason never intended to shoot anyone, been playing a sick joke of which he and I became the butts? I could have asked Darrell—*Were there shells in that gun?*—and he would have said yes. No matter what he'd seen. The thought sat in my stomach, a rotting fish.

I stare out the window of a 737 between Albuquerque and St. Louis, my gut punched through to my spine. I've been dreading everything about this trip. My wife squeezes my arm, and my trance breaks as the wheels touch the runway.

Darrell was a hospital corpsman in the Navy, and afterward became an emergency room nurse. Three nights ago, ER staff were treating an already-paranoid meth addict found half-frozen on the streets. The man came unglued, wrested a gun from a security guard. Darrell pushed an intern out of the way. The bullet ruptured his aorta.

I'm a pallbearer. So is Scott.

I've seen Scott no more than a half-dozen times in the past thirty-six years, exchanged nothing more than brief, meaningless small talk, studiously avoiding words like *dog* and *poacher*. I've always blamed him for what happened, for the torment that has stayed on my heels all these years. If he hadn't been such an ass about shooting that dog. That day can pop into my head at any time, appear out of nowhere, with no trigger I can discern.

Coveralls covered in blood and grime. Shovels hitting the ground. Darrell's frown telling me I might have killed someone for no reason. Now and then, the torment is present when I wake in the morning. I'm glad I never remember my dreams.

"Wish you two would fix this," Marie once said to me.

But we didn't fix anything. In my mind, Scott walked away from that day unscathed. A day set loose on me like an avalanche. I didn't get to walk away at all. I never left those woods.

It's been a long time, some might say too long, to carry the resentment. And I've adjusted, learned to dampen the memories before they break the surface. But Darrell's death, the way he died, has dredged them up. The memories and the resentment are closer to the surface today. Much closer.

But maybe it's not as simple as I prefer to believe.

"I could have stopped him," Darrell once said when Scott's name came up. "It didn't seem important. It never occurred to me it might lead anywhere the way it did."

I changed the subject. Because there's another side of the torment. What if I hadn't been too spineless to stand up to Scott? Maybe it hadn't mattered to Darrell. But I didn't want Scott to shoot that dog. I didn't stop him either. And then I used that same gun.

There wasn't any choice. No. There were choices, and we made them. Scott made a choice to shoot a dog. I made a choice to not stop him.

I tell myself I'm not who I was then. The person I am today would tell Scott to put the gun away, to stop being a jackass. But it doesn't change the past. And if I truly believe I am someone else now, isn't it possible the same is true of Scott? When my sister called with the news, she relayed something Marie told her. When Scott found out, he ransacked a trunk in their basement until he found an old pistol he hadn't touched in more than thirty years. He handed it to their son. "Get rid of it. Destroy it, bury it eight feet in the ground, drop it in eighty feet of water out at Devil's Kitchen, I don't care. Just make sure nobody can ever use it again."

My sister didn't understand, but I doubt Marie intended the message for her.

We leave the plane looking for my sister, who is supposed to meet us. Then I see Scott waiting outside the gate. Marie nudges him and he glances up, catches my eye for a moment with a glazed, faraway look. The same lost look of thirty-six years ago. A look I'm forced to admit I understand.

I'm not the only one still in those woods.

We have a friend to bury tomorrow. Then perhaps it's long past time Scott and I attend to the consequences of some choices we once made, try to find a path out of those woods before the way is blocked forever. If he's willing. If I'm willing. We aren't who we were then. Surely, we cannot be who we were then.

_____

John Mummert grew up in Illinois, both in the suburbs of Chicago and the southern part of the state. He spent thirty years in the water quality protection and restoration field, the majority of that time with the state environmental agency in Texas. He has since turned his attention to writing, with an emphasis on historical fiction. He currently lives in the Dallas-Fort Worth area. "Who We Were Then" is his first fiction publication.

AND NOW A WORD FROM BAMBI'S MOTHER
by Cepa Onion

I'm so flipping happy.

The thought flies like a streamer as I watch my unseatbelted self shoot through my car windshield. At the same time, my lipstick-red Porsche splatters like a paintball across the tunnel wall.

That's when I know I'm dead. Have to be. How else could I watch myself and my beautiful, now-flambéed car rest in pieces? Laughter shakes me like a wet dog.

"Rest in pieces," I muse out loud. But how can I be laughing at a time like this? I wonder if I'm still under the influence of the four margaritas. Part of lunch on a hell-hot Arizona day at a downtown Italian-Mexican hybrid restaurant.

Even if I am under the influence, that "rest in pieces" line is too funny. I know I stole it from some Halloween decoration. But I still want to share it with the other sales guys.

I say sales guys because that's what most of us are. I, on the other hand, am a rare sales gal. One of nine women on an eighty-eight-person team. We sell pharmaceuticals. I make an ideal female sales package.

Playing off my name, Helen, I christened myself Helen of Troy: whose ass could launch a thousand sales.

Selling pharmaceuticals is really cool. Especially if you overlook the side effects. God, I love my job—or loved it. I guess it's all past-tense now. I'm really going to miss it. And the money. The money was to die for. I chortle again.

Okay, that isn't funny. I'm just stress-laughing now. Because, like I say, I'm dead. I can somehow feel it. If that's really the case, why am I still here? And why is all of this so hilarious? Can a dead person still be drunk? For eternity? Wow, wouldn't that be great?

My heart soars as I look down at my translucent self. I'm overjoyed to notice I'm still clad in my strapless royal blue dress. The perfect final resting outfit. I love the way it clings to my forty-year-old figure-eight shape, barely skimming my taut derrière.

Lit by my observation, I peer at the ambulance and fire truck light show: Vivid reds and blues slice the air, intertwined with a cacophony of sirens. All for me? So flattering.

I watch the EMTs ply my mangled body with bandages and tubes until it becomes boring. I yawn at them all. I'm relieved to find no innocent victims smeared next to me. Just one guilty one, who is now floating above the wreckage. Wait—why am I still here? Shouldn't I be moving on? To the next level? I went to Sunday School. I know what's supposed to happen.

Suddenly, my gaze lands on the amber chunks dotting the pavement like blood-soaked rock candy. I zoom in. Oh my God, they can't be. But they are: my pulverized implants. I can't count the number of sales those helped me snag. I'm going to miss them, too. Why won't I hurry up and cross over?

"Hey! Hello?! Can anybody hear me?" I scream at the throng of firefighters. I even swoop over to them and kick their uniformed butts. Instead of reacting, they blast water at the orange flames twisting from my crumpled Porsche. So much smoke, but I can't smell it—or anything, for that matter. Must have something to do with being dead. Or maybe...almost dead.

Why did I have that fourth margarita? I know, I felt the sale depended on it. And it worked, didn't it? Didn't I close the deal right after getting the five hospital guys to laugh by sharing my liquor-induced insight about how all mothers suck except for the dead ones?

"By the very nature of the job, you're set up to fail. No one can do what's expected of a mother and still be human," I proclaimed, wagging a salsa-drenched breadstick in the air. I may have even been standing at that point, holding court over my blurry-eyed subjects. "Ever notice how all the good mothers die in the movies?" I continued. "Get them out of the way before the first spanking. Like Bambi's mother. You know, the doe that hunter killed right after the opening credits, way back in the forties? Bambi's mother started it all."

I can speak with authority on the subject. Since I, too, am a mother.

A fit of giggles rises and then chokes into a hard sob. Because I can't believe I am just now thinking of my precious jewel, the chip off the old ovary: my only son, Marc.

I gave birth to Marc when I was twenty. I never knew who his father was. "How could I know? It was a really great week." I used to spew that line, even in front of Marc, who always smiled at my little joke. We were close like that. So simpatico. More like friends, really.

And boy, did we need to be.

My father, a furious obstetrician, and my mother, an equally incensed country club tennis coach, had no patience for my getting pregnant. They threw poor little rich me out of their lives. But it was a soft landing. Because to ensure I stayed away, they bought me a condominium. I even enjoyed a good-riddance allowance. When your family has money, the world's your pearl. No messy oyster required. After finishing college, courtesy of my trust fund and a million nannies for Marc, I started in sales, catapulting into the embarrassingly lucrative world of pharmaceuticals.

I used to joke that Marc was raised like the Prince of Wales. Because I outsourced everything and only saw him on holidays, whenever I wasn't too busy, that is. Marc understood my priorities from day one.

I remember doting on him for about thirty minutes in the hospital after his too-easy birth. I looked into his pruney red face, under his damp black hair, and fell for him. But after that first half-hour, I grew bored. I flirted with the orderlies just to make things more interesting, and I happily chucked Marc into the nursery so I could suck down grilled cheese and watch Cops. Marc looked at me with his Bambi-brown eyes and seemingly understood I had more pressing needs. Sure, I breastfed him, but only because I liked the way the milk augmented me like a porn star. That inspired me to get my now-smashed-to-bits implants.

But Marc has become every parent's dream. All the lessons and boarding schools I piled on him paid huge dividends. He's off at college in Colorado now, no doubt triple-majoring in architecture, philosophy, and Spanish literature. Not to mention wowing everyone as the star of the college diving team. Too busy saving the world as part of groups like Engineers Without Borders to venture home. That's why I haven't talked to him in three years.

Now, cloistered in the cold tunnel amid the bustle of firefighters, cops, and EMTs, I sit on the pavement, which oddly chills my rear end. Then a big blast of insight hits me. I know why I'm not transforming. Unlike Bambi's dead mother, I've been given the chance to say goodbye to my son.

I know what I have to do.

I fly into Marc's apartment. I don't mean to get there so fast; it's just how things apparently work in the afterlife. One minute, I'm mulling over the logistics of traveling from Arizona to Marc's college in Colorado, straining to remember how they do it in movies. In the next compressed second, I slam onto the floor of a dark, hazy room.

I immediately recognize my precious Marc. He has my same superb cheekbones and ringlet curls. So handsome. Even in this gray air, anyone can see that. Why is it so dark in here? Isn't it still afternoon?

And this dump can't possibly be Marc's apartment. Clothes drape the apathetic furniture like melting Salvador Dalí clocks, while a stack of grease-drenched pizza boxes stands guard in one corner. And is that really an orange-and-blue bong? Next to a pile of soiled underclothes? Thank God my new form prevents me from smelling anything.

I scan the hovel, looking for the off-color roommates who obviously caused this wreckage. Although perfect himself, Marc always surrounded himself with questionable friends. Unable to see anyone else, I slither closer to get a better look at my son.

Marc's perched almost arrogantly on the center cushion of a faded yellow corduroy sofa. A wall-sized flat-screen TV illuminates an animated scene of soldiers and terrorists blasting each other bloody. He maneuvers the action on the screen with a fancy game-controller-thing. Every so often, the action freezes and the words "Terrorists win" or "Counter-terrorists win" reverberate from the monstrosity. While he clicks, Marc talks into white earbuds that drip from his ears like mini walrus tusks.

My son wears a moth-chewed tan T-shirt, along with low-cut, gang-banger blue jeans splashed with stains that look like bleach and something green. Upon closer inspection, I notice that his precious licorice-black ringlets glisten with grease, and his gaunt face needs a shave. Who is this? I feel as if the universe is playing a trick on me.

I blink hard and open my eyes, hoping this silly layabout changeling will turn back into my golden child.

But the anti-Marc is still there, talking in a too-deep telephone voice about how he can't wait to get there to "defend his fucking title." Title? Excitement spears me. He's defending a title? I'll bet it's diving.

"He thinks he can fucking beat me? No way. Not today, not *mañana*. I been zoning for two fucking months."

On and on blathers Marc's deep, dark "F-ing" conversation, while the video game terrorists and good guys explode to red. I stand off to the side, teeming with fury. Too bad no one can see or feel me, because I really want to beat the crap out of Marc. Finally, he clicks off the video game. In one fluid motion, he stands and scoops a Pikachu-encased cellphone off the plywood coffee table. He stuffs it into his back pocket and shuffles toward the front door, lobbing a million F-bombs into his earbuds along the way.

I can't take it anymore.

"Enough of the language, Marc," I yell as I sail over and raise my hand to smack his stupid head. To my utter, out-of-body surprise, Marc looks right at me. His eyes bulge like boiled eggs and lock onto me. He scrambles backward like a crab escaping the pelican of death. Then he spins, claws at the doorknob, and bolts out the door.

"You can see me!" I repeat, overjoyed. Because he obviously does, and he must know I'm a spirit. In real life, he'd never be afraid of me.

Marc bounds down the apartment hallway so fast and erratically I think of pinball. As I chase him, I ring with euphoria, because I realize I had it wrong. I'm not here to say goodbye. I'm here to help Marc reach his true potential. With all the power of Bambi's idealized mother, I vow to tough-love my Marc back into shape.

He stops outside, standing on a grassy area alongside the apartment parking lot. He leans forward, rests a hand on a fat tree, and breathes as if about to break. I hover next to him. Finally, he looks at me.

"Oh God, how I've missed you," I say, beaming.

"Holy shit! Y-y-you're a-a-a fu—"

"Stop the language!" I shout in his face. "I'm dead, all right? I did something stupid, wrecked the car, and died."

"Dead?"

"Yeah. Game over. But now, I can be the mother I didn't have time to be. We can have a real-life do-over."

Marc shakes his head.

I launch into how much I love him: his sensitive eyes, his sweet disposition, that one time at age five when he scored high on an IQ test.

Marc doesn't seem to hear. He's suddenly too busy ninja-chopping my stomach while machine-gunning hysterical, high-pitched giggles.

"Quit that!" I ball my hand. I want to punch him but stop, reminding myself that's not what good mothers do.

"Fucking trippy," he says, shoving his hands into his front pockets and walking away with purpose. He must have disconnected his "F-ing" phone call because he's no longer blathering into his earbuds.

"Nice place you have," I say like a polite stranger, gliding alongside him. "Sorry I never visited. So do you like any of your classes this year?"

"My mom's a ghost," he mutters. "What the fuck?" Still walking, he appears almost amused now.

"Where are we going? You said something about defending a title? It's for diving, right? You always looked so graceful in those videos the swim club sent me." He looks at me then pulls his gaze away, plowing onward.

I strive to match his impressive pace. "Oh, by the way, I left you lots of money. But if you keep ordering pizza the way it appears you are, it won't last. After this title thing, let's sit down and work out a budget, okay?"

Marc ignores me, and we continue. Down dirt roads, around bear-proof garbage bins, past deep blue ponds and through clumps of evergreens, whose wintergreen scent I struggle to smell. Then without warning, some sort of outdoor festival springs up like a mirage. Percolating with laughter and cheers, so many beautiful empty-faced young people revel around a pile of massive tents, concession stands, and a ragtag rock band, made worse by a blown speaker.

Some crater-faced boy, who resembles Shaggy from *Scooby Doo*, meanders toward Marc. He's probably the same age. But everything about his flip-flop, hunched-over self says loser. I make a mental note to obliterate this friendship ASAP.

"Hey! You made it, bro," Shaggy Lookalike calls, ambling closer, stoner-slow. The bong in Marc's apartment obviously belongs to this mutant. "When you screamed like a girl and hung up, I freaked."

"Yeah, sorry about that." Without further comment, they execute an elaborate hand-punch series.

"Hey Tom," Marc says, his eyes on me. "Can I ask you something weird? You don't see a ghost next to me, do you?"

Tom looks right through me. I hold my breath.

"What kind of ghost?" Tom asks like a moron.

"Never mind," Marc says.

I exhale.

"C'mon, Marc," I interject. "You're not really friends with this guy, are you? You're so much better than this. What about history? Have you taken any history classes yet? You always liked the History Channel."

Marc turns away without an answer. Then he and Tom shuffle into a long line of man-boys snaking into a ginormous white tent. While they wait, they yammer on about how Tom has gotten seven hundred dollars in bets, and how "fucking wonderful" that is because Marc is "so fucking primed to win it all."

Despite Loser Boy and all the cussing, pride swells in me. It's such a long line. Whatever title Marc holds must have been hard-fought. No one in line appears very athletic, so it's probably not for diving. It must be a competition of the minds—like chess. Marc was always such a Renaissance man. I stand a little taller as we trudge forward.

When we reach the entryway, I see a sign announcing what Marc's going to do. My hopes drop like granny breasts. I sigh.

Marc and Tom enter the packed tent. They cut through the crowd, and Marc takes a seat at a long table draped in white. There, he's joined by several other male idiots, who all share the carefree look of adult dependency. I slide up to Marc and park my butt on the table right in front of him like a challenge.

"A hotdog-eating contest?" I ask. "This is your *title*? Eating hotdogs?"

"Just shut up," he says.

"Don't talk to your mother like that."

"Don't talk to me. At all," he says.

"C'mon, Marc, this isn't the real you. Let's go back to Arizona. You can take an aptitude test and find out what you'd like to study."

Marc shakes his head, deliberate and mean. He looks at the ground, the table, the audience, everywhere but me. Some fool in a chef suit begins sliding rows of hotdogs onto the contestants' ivory plates. He makes a special point of announcing Marc as the defending champion, to which a chorus of drunks in the audience boom their hefty approval.

Then the chef suit guy fires what appears to be a real pistol. To cheers and jeers, Marc gets on it, swallowing so much I think of a boa constrictor.

"Slow down! You're going to hurt yourself!" I plead as he crams hotdogs into his mouth.

Masculine cheers pound the room, and chef clones fill the contestants' plates anew.

"Stop it!" I scream. "Can't you see? I made you this way. I ruined you, because I wasn't there. This isn't how you should be."

"Yes, it is!" he chokes. Then just like that, my Marc gasps. After a few airless seconds, he turns blue and flops off his chair. His skull hits the ground hard and fast. The crowd blanches and inhales in unison.

"No!" I cry, propelling myself next to Marc's face. The chef who fired the gun transforms into a responsible-looking grown-up and runs to my son's side. There, he executes the perfect Heimlich maneuver. But it's no use. Marc remains unresponsive.

"Call an ambulance," the chef orders some bystander before launching into proficient CPR.

A clump of idiot boys laugh, apparently not quite grasping what occurred.

Oh no. This can't be happening. Not now. I lean my head close to Marc's beautiful, now-azure, face and scream-beg him to live. "Come on, Marc. Breathe! You can't die. You have your whole life ahead, and now you have a real mom, who's finally gonna be there. The way I should have but wasn't. I'm here now. Please. Don't. Die."

After what seems like a few chaotic seconds, but must have been much longer, a transparent form rises from Marc's cold, stiff body. Just like I did in the tunnel.

Marc looks around, as if to get his bearings. He peers down at his see-through body, then looks at me.

"Whoops," he mutters.

No. I refuse to accept he's dead. I have to fix this. But how? Marc won't listen to me.

Oh God, what can I do? I channel all the goodness of Bambi's mother for answers, and that does the trick. Just like one of those old Polaroids, the perfect solution comes into focus: reverse psychology. I'll fool Marc into choosing life by acting like I want him to do the opposite.

Without another stupid thought, I sail over and wrap Marc in a hard hug.

"Isn't this great?" I sing-song. "Now that you're dead, we can hang out. Oh Marc, don't you see? We'll be together. Forever and ever. Through all of eternity. Won't that be wonderful?"

Marc's eyes widen, and he spins away from me. Without looking back, he launches himself headfirst back into his body.

I knew he was a great diver.

———————

Susan Schooleman (pen name Cepa Onion) wrote for Hollywood TV before trading that career in for parenthood. She's been published by Samuel French and Self, and in 2019 was a winner in the Rocky Mountain Fiction Writers Colorado Gold Contest for her women's fiction novel Staying Sane in the Carpool Lane.

This piece gives a different twist to the idealized,

mythical mom who gets killed off early in a story (à la Bambi) and underscores how the power of parental love endures, no matter how imperfect.

AN OCCURRENCE IN FARWAY CANYON
by Stephen Hillard

At the edge of nowhere in the lost canyon lands of the American West, a grim gust of sirocco wind rattled the sheet metal roof of the abandoned diner called The Eat. It was unusual for this time of year, and it foretold the arrival of change.

Inside the diner, the last remnants of the Heavy Gang—Mose, Darlus, and Tector—were gathered. The time for this meeting always came in October. Every October. This year. The year before. On and on as far back as they could remember—which, for them, was an ambitious task. Their memories were hazy. Like squinting blearily into a smeared and foggy bottle to check for that one last drop of recollection.

What they did know, felt really, was that somehow things were not the same. Even Old Mose, the most silent man of a silent, almost somnambulant crew, seemed to be waking up. As if achy feet were coming alive after a long walk in dreamtime.

Darlus, the Vietnam vet, was surly, like his self of decades ago. Tector, the tag-along wingman, had inexplicably changed the coffee last week to a gourmet blend. He had started playing odd, up-tempo classic rock on the jukebox. *Born to be Wild* replacing *Sleepwalk*.

Little things.

Tectonic changes compared to the last fifty years.

But the biggest disruption had just walked in the door. The visiting SteenCo representative. This year he was new—a trim youngster, pure Silicon Valley, complete with khakis, blue monogrammed polo shirt, and designer shades that he was just now removing with a smooth, almost rehearsed effect. Out west here, he might be called the SteenCo Kid.

Missing from his side was Doc Sevrin, the elderly, bifocaled hack of a government doctor who dithered and told the same lame jokes ("There was this here farmer's daughter"). His one job had been to give them their annual "prevention shots." In his place lurked a security man. Part bouncer, maybe ex-SEAL, pure bad attitude. He stood behind the SteenCo Kid, hands hidden in bulgy jacket pockets, compiling situational awareness and sizing up the three occupants of stools and booths spread around The Eat.

The Kid studied the old men before him and then looked directly at Mose. "Like I said, go in there and get the damn diary."

Darlus couldn't hold back. "Wait! Just a damn second. Why? Why *now*?" He leaned forward, scooting to the edge of the bench seat.

The security man eased to the side, covering Darlus from a clear angle. Tector moved behind the counter. There, next to him, rested a vintage balance scale. The kind with a pedestal, a central beam, and opposing pans on each end. Perhaps once the pride of a long-departed cook who actually measured meat and cheese and bread dough—before the place was shut down with an hour's notice.

Tector scowled and removed his beat-up, Longhorn-emblemed, shit-kicker baseball hat and hung it on the scales.

The Kid sensed the repositioning around him and the need for defusing this unexpected reaction. "Look, this is nothing…really. Some new information has come up. An old letter surfaced from some old archives. The company needs to…corroborate it." He paused again. "Just checking."

Before Darlus could object again, the Kid reached out a pale, patronizing hand and placed it on Mose's shoulder. "They say you were the crew boss. You know where to go. And what to avoid." His hand opened to show a piece of paper. "Combination. Office safe."

Mose looked up with rheumy eyes.

Crew boss.

The words stung as much as ever. But the Kid had a point. He had put his finger on the one button that could still motivate Mose.

A coffee cup crashed to the floor as Darlus pushed his feet outside the booth and stood up. Tector removed his hands from the countertop and let them down, perhaps reaching for something more than a big weaponized spoon.

Mr. Security took a calculated step back and nestled his right hand in his coat pocket. A low hum filled the air. The rising tension felt flammable, like a leaky propane tank getting ready to erupt in a ball of flame.

Mose put his head down, as if focusing on something deep and unsettling.

Tector lifted his right hand, armed, sure enough, with a big metal ladle. He slammed it down on the counter. It got away and flew across the room. The pans hanging off each end of the beam on the Toledo balance scale swayed until one fell off. The beam tipped completely over to one side. *Thunk.*

Tector stammered. "Da-damn it. It's dead out there and b-been that way. Sealed up tight. They even emptied out the p-postal station before they b-burned it down that night. No one's been in there since…"

The Kid held his hands up, stepping back as if his security man might have to take over. His face said he never expected crap from this sleepy little crew in this obscure canyon hiding the long-shuttered SteenCo Mill. A place that harbored its secrets like a tomb. The seconds stretched out, becoming a phalanx of threatening spears that surrounded them all. Everyone waited for someone to make a move.

In the quiet, Mose's voice was low but clear. "I'll go," he said. "I'll go. Alone."

His teeth clenched, leaving the reason unsaid. *After all, I was the crew boss.* Wind rattled the sheet metal again, bringing to Farway Canyon the tang of moisture and the distant scent of wet sagebrush. The storm darkened the horizon and loomed over the forgotten place found on no published map.

Three hours later, the words *crew boss* still tumbling like rough stones in his mind, Mose pulled up his collar against the breeze. He was scared even as he marveled at the novel feeling of his heart trip-hammering in his chest. He stood at the threshold to the main building of the SteenCo Mill. Worn brick walls soared three stories above him, their broken windows looking out like dead eyes at the distant security ramparts. A low wind seethed along the wall, whispering of old ghosts and long-ago catastrophes.

Mose touched the oak door in front of him. Its riveted planks were buckled, and it canted slightly off its hinges. It squealed as he pushed it open.

No sneaking in, he thought. *Whatever's here knows anyway.*

He stepped past the threshold and entered another world.

A last beam of westering light, perhaps cut from beneath the vault of storm clouds, peeked over his shoulder and shot into the building. Just as quickly it disappeared, swallowed by a thicket of blackness. He cringed and swept the flashlight about like a rapier. Familiar objects flashed before him. Number Five forklift, unmanned and still waiting. A cluster of fifty-five-gallon drums, one hatted with a lunchpail and coffee cup. Tools, scattered as if cast aside. A chain ascending to a ceiling beyond the reach of his light. A few dust motes cycling about wildly as if some presence had just slipped away from the space.

He took a deep breath and scrunched his nose at the alchemy of smells. Acrid rust, grease and oil, chemicals long resigned to neglect, bird dung layered in iron joists far above. Something lurked beneath the rest of the smells. A dank, almost imperceptible odor that was somehow fresh.

He turned his head to advantage his good ear. Ticks. A clock, somewhere? Tiny clinks. Tank rivets adjusting? Wings flapping far away. Tiger birds nesting far overhead? A scurry. Perhaps in all this time, the rats had mutated to terrier size.

As he peered into the nave of this dark cathedral of abandoned industry, a familiar feeling settled over Mose. Unlike the rest of his emotions, this one had refused to become foggy with time. In fact, over the years it had grown, becoming an unbearable weight that ruled his days. Pretty much every day, year after year. Now it grew even heavier. He was *so* close to the place of his original sin. The crucible. The yellow cake vat.

The room where it rested was one floor down, thirty feet below him. He recalled the details, testing for the millionth time if just maybe his memory was missing some exculpatory item. Maybe there was still some tiny piece of mitigating evidence. He could go see.

It's right there...just down the stairs.

His practical side flinched. *No way. Get this done. Get your rear out of here.*

A mind-echo came bouncing back. *Out to what?*

He hated that kind of question. One that just might demand a Big Answer. Fifty years, and the answer sheet of his life was still blank. The one emotion he felt, the unpadded, unrelieved weight, was as fresh as ever.

Guilt.

It wasn't supposed to be this way. Growing up beneath big puffy clouds that sailed on knockout blue skies over gentle green woods, his heart had nurtured a burning premonition of happiness. He trusted true north and he trusted tomorrow.

Life, unfortunately, didn't get the memo. Drugs, a busted marriage, a kid he got to see twice a year if he was current on his support, and, finally, the long path to this moment.

Fifty years ago he got this job at the SteenCo Mill. A job he didn't deserve and wasn't prepared for. Compliments of his foreman uncle putting in a good word with the union and sticking it to the mucky-mucks upstairs. He became the crew boss, telling hard men twice his age how to do things he'd never done before.

And then came the Accident.

After that, love, aspiration, family, hope. They had all seeped away. Now he was sealed up, just like this mill. Guilt trudged inside him, and it trudged alone.

He took a rag from his pocket, removed his hardhat, and wiped sweat from his forehead. He sensed that, outside, the end-of-day clock was spinning madly to a stormy conclusion. Lightning glanced off the beams and broken windows far overhead. Deep moans of thunder vibrated in his boots and seemed to come from the very bowels of the Mill, like a restless dragon.

He had to be back on the road within the hour. Down that windy, eroded track to the chain-link electric fence topped with brambles of razor wire. The electronic gate would be sealed soon, leaving him to whatever demons might roam this storm-fevered night.

He looked up and peered beyond his flashlight's wavering reach. His goal, the office, had to be just ahead, around a cluster of tanks and across the mill floor.

He cleared the first tank and jumped back as his flashlight revealed what looked like a swarm of anacondas. In the wavering, scattershot beam, they seemed to writhe.

Only his memory saved him. His mind frantically assembled the pieces until the imagery became coherent.

The building, he recalled, had been a sugar mill until it was rebuilt in the frenzied Cold War uranium boom of the 1950s. So frenzied that when they lacked a supply of metal pipes, they made do with government surplus—in this case, huge naval wharf hoses.

He stepped gingerly over them. A few of them dove down a stairwell. Down to where the Accident happened.

It was 1968. The yellow cake vat down there was a wide, twenty-foot-deep cauldron where refined uranium was gathered. From time to time it had to be mucked out and the outlet at the bottom cleaned. A new ore, called Steenium, was being run through the Mill. When refined, it turned into a greenish, high-viscosity goo. It had clogged the vat.

The Heavy Gang, labor-pool vets with missing fingers and attitudes as creased as their faces, got the assignment. Two new kids, Darlus and Tector, had just joined them.

Mose wondered what any of this could have to do with this mysterious diary. A book of petty secrets? Prom date adventures? What could be worth sending him back *here*?

His thoughts pivoted back to the present as light glinted straight ahead. Probably his flashlight reflecting on the glass windows of the office, a glorified overseer's perch that sat on a platform overlooking the main floor. He moved toward the platform and surprised himself as he pulled the .45 six-shooter from his belt and let it lead the way, the flashlight beam accompanying its aim.

'Course, nothing in here is gonna be scared of my little pop-gun.

The stairs leading up to the office were as he expected, no footprints in the accumulated dust. He stepped up gingerly, surveying ahead, down, sideways with swaths of tepid light that seemed to be fading by the minute. He whacked the flashlight with his hand, but it didn't help.

The door to the office was wide open, as if flung aside in panicked departure. He spent a moment looking at the company logo overhead, along with a big radioactivity sign with a hand-scrawled smiley on it. A big "Safety First" display stood by the door. Now streaked and discolored, it bragged about "SteenCo Sets A New Record: 543 Days Without An Accident."

His heart ached as he stared at the display. Eight guys sucked down into the vat and presumed dead sure kiboshed that.

Another rumble of thunder jittered the steel platform. Mose stepped inside the office. It housed a couple of desks, file cabinets, some blueprints that drooped off the wall. An open lunchbox displayed its contents of chewed paper and mice poop. A face that Mose knew looked at him from the wall. It was framed in a front-page newspaper article. The person was forty-ish, with a modest, innocent expression. The headline read, "Billionaire Prospector Charles Steen Announces Discovery Of New Kind Of Ore." The word "Steenium" in the body of the article had been circled in something that had faded to a sad hint of green.

So long ago. Charlie Steen was long since departed. Right after the Accident, he'd left a note that said he was going out to the Mill. He was never heard from again. His truck was found outside the same building Mose was in now. The surviving members of the Heavy Gang were told to haul the truck away and no need to go poking around further.

Later there was a whispered story, probably invented by the SteenCo tin hats to cover things up. Supposedly, Charlie had been heard from. He'd gone out to Vegas to squander what remained of his prospecting riches and retired to some beach far over the horizon.

Mose's mind-movie replayed the moment. "Suurre," he had said as they sat around The Eat back in '69. Right after their first set of "prevention shots."

Tector had looked out from under his baseball cap, the same one he was wearing today. "What'd he do, walk a hundred miles out of these canyons? My money says Steen never came outta the Mill."

Darlus had stared out the diner window, studying a pair of orange-and-black striped birds. After a long moment, he chimed in, "Tiger birds. They never come this far from the Mill. Something's disturbed them."

That desultory exchange became typical of their slow-motion conversations. Vacuous words, often repeated verbatim, perhaps taking years rather than minutes as the foggy dreamtime of their existence settled in.

They should have retired long ago, gotten their final two-week pay, and been sent on their way. Instead, they had been kept on. The only eyewitnesses to the Accident. Their paychecks kept coming. The annual shots were duly administered. The checks said "SteenCo," but they vaguely suspected it was some sort of government front.

"My watchdogs," the visiting company man said each year, almost patting them on the head as Doc Sevrin went to work on them.

The Doc always seemed to be in on some secret, chatting to them in lullaby sing-song as he filled each syringe, swabbed each of their arms, and held up each needle so that it glinted wickedly in the light. "This will protect you from the, uh, low-level radiation you got way back then." Pop. In went the needle. "Just a precaution, no need to worry."

Suurre.

Whatever was in that shot kept them in a perpetual fuzz.

But hey, a paycheck is a paycheck. So they stayed on, hanging out at The Eat near the main gate, lingering in that accumulating fog bank of years with nothing much happening. Getting older. Low-rent Rip Van Winkles.

Until recently. And now the Doc failed to show up for his house call. It was strange to feel oneself waking up after fifty years. Mental eyes blinking and looking back at all that time. At…nothing. No places visited, no family, no doing, no dancing. No living. All Mose had felt was that ball and chain of guilt.

The rumble again. Lightning flashed in the upper stories and projected long shadows into the depths of the Mill.

Hell, get on with this!

Mose began to look for what he'd come for. On a desk, beneath a pile of blueprints, he found a small safe. He cleared off the scrolls and knelt, both knees popping. *Getting up will be the hard part*, he thought. He studied the dial and hand lever. "Vulcan," presumably the brand, was engraved on it in quaint 19th-century lettering with fiery filigrees. It could've been a prop in old Western movies.

He put down the pistol, balanced the dimming flashlight on the desk, fished the piece of paper with the combination from his coveralls, set the lever to perpendicular, and rotated the dial clockwise three times to clear the tumblers. It resisted at first but then seemed to relax. Six tries and something clunked inside. He turned the handle up and felt the door loosen.

Inside the safe rested three items: a check ledger, a dented petty cash box, and a leather-covered book with a ratty cord wrapped around it. He pulled the book out. Not exactly a diary. The cover read:

C Steen
Prospector's Journal

He flipped through pages of technical entries, locations, names and phone numbers, geologic notations, drawings. A note about visiting Disneyland. A long series of entries about the atomic structure of heavy elements, such as uranium.

When he got to the last page, a typed letter fell out.

It was dated the day after the Accident. At the top, an agitated hand-scrawl read:

Just in case something happens, I left a copy of this letter at the Farway postal station, addressed to SteenCo corporate.

The body of the letter read:

October 12, 1968

You fools won't listen. Steenium isn't just a uranium-like ore. It is an extremely heavy element, beyond what physicists say should exist. So far down the periodic table that even the blank spaces are classified. Its properties are unknown.

Correction: were unknown.

Here is the truth that is being hidden in this project: While prospecting, I found this ore in a single deposit behind a wall hidden in a cleft in a nearby canyon. The surface of the wall was a rough mud plaster, eroded but still showing petroglyphs made by Folsom-point-era hunters. The glyphs, it turns out, were probably warnings.

Beneath that surface was a smooth wall material carbon-dated at 200,000 years.

We had to dynamite the wall along its edges. Inside we found Steenium interspersed with a dense carbon-like material, like uranium cores are mixed with graphite to slow down and weaken the radioactive process. To keep them asleep, as it were.

The bottom line: Steenium (I wish I hadn't named it) was deposited here eons ago by somebody. Your guess as to who, or what, they might be.

My guess is that it gets worse. I believe this stuff was placed here, on this obscure blue ball, not because it was valuable. Just the opposite. It is probably the most dangerous substance in the universe. Put that in capital letters.

It turns out Earth is an intergalactic toxic waste dump.

And yesterday we undid Steenium's prison. We refined it back to its pure, undiluted strength. Back to the level where it becomes sentient, diabolical, cunning, and increasingly mobile. And mind-controlling.

We woke it up.

Even with the years of silent neglect, the words seemed to twitch with a wild, blithering insanity. As if Charlie's mental easy chair was lifting completely off its rockers.

Except Mose felt it was as true as day and night, as regret, as remorse, as the guilt he carried on his back every day.

Gazing at the last page, he replayed his own fateful moment: six guys from the Heavy Gang down in the vat, already up to their knees in the weird gooey stuff, mucking it up in buckets. Complaining that *this shit is weird, man.*

Instead of pulling the crew out, Mose ordering more of them down into the vat. Darlus and Tector telling him to shove it and climbing out to run up the stairway. Mose getting pissed like a petty tin hat and not paying attention as the goo started to climb up the sides and encase the men in the vat.

They never got out. Only their screams, increasingly muffled, bounced off Mose as he skedaddled up the stairs. He cut and ran, and never looked back.

Out of all the foggy nothing that had swallowed up his life, Mose remembered this one moment in high resolution. The sharp pain in his shin as he slipped and banged it running up the stairs. The surreal sound floating out of his mouth. The Heavy Gang's screams echoing up the stairwell. He remembered the whole damn thing with condemning, crystalline clarity.

He even knew its weight. His soul could calculate the heaviness of his guilt as precisely as that Toledo balance scale on the counter at The Eat.

In a kind of free association, perhaps his mind loosening from the grip of Doc Sevrin's mind-control drug, he pondered that balance scale. Tilting and grossly overweighed on one side. Not even the weight of truth could right the balance. But perhaps, just maybe, something else could.

An idea, high and wild, swirled dizzily in his head. His mind jacked through an array of excuses to justify backing away from it: the storm, the late hour, his mission, Let It Go, whatever.

He set the journal on top of the safe and headed out the office door. He made his way to the main floor and the stairway leading down to the yellow cake vat, the last known abode of pure Steenium. There he hesitated.

If a hand could put squeeze marks into steel, Mose did it as he gripped the handrail. After a moment, he extended his leg and pointed the toe of his boot like a clumsy ballerina. He took a first cautious step down. Before him was a pool of darkness that defied his flashlight.

He took one more step, then another. Still time to retreat.

The stairs came to a landing and doglegged back down. He got to the landing and turned to ponder the last ten steps.

A sound, a smushy footstep from below. A squish, like jelly beneath a bare foot. Something was there. Some*things*, actually. They were waiting.

Here was the defining moment, all over again. Like way back then, he could turn and cut and run.

The weight of guilt seemed like it would buckle his legs and crush him then and there, robbing him of any decision. But it didn't. It seemed to lift just a little. Another step, and Mose felt the strangest thing. For once in so long, he could sense who he was and decide what he would do.

A faint smell of green leaves waving below puffy clouds in a knockout blue sky came to him.

He turned to fully square with the stairs. His feeble flashlight died in his hand.

A greenish glow with no apparent source began to slowly pulse in the air. It showed vague forms just beyond the last step. They were moving toward him in a slow-mo, lurching cluster. They raised their arms. Their mouths opened, as if about to speak his name and say "Old Friend." Their faces and hands had a glowing sheen. Even encased in green goo, they were still recognizable. The original Heavy Gang, coming up to reintroduce themselves and bestow their greetings. Maybe even say, "Good to see you, Boss."

He could feel truth swirling in the air. The moment was alive and pulsing with never-imagined possibilities. He could go down now and meet them. Perhaps commune in their greater sense of being. Merge into their guiltless realm.

They were coming up the steps. Open to him. They were his crew, greenish and slimed, yes, but still unaged.

Another stair step closer. He could take their approaching jumble of extended green hands into his own, let them embrace him. Feel their kindred thoughts.

Without knowing its name, he realized he could join the Steenium Mind. Relish and absorb its post-sanity clarity. He could participate in sentience in its purest, most democratic form. A cosmic crowdsourcing from across endless galaxies and countless light years of gathering conscious minds like his.

Evil? Diabolical? Charlie Steen was so wrong. Mose knew that, all in all, Steenium was good.

The first gooey fingertips reached out and crept across his face. His fingers intertwined with theirs. He felt their grip, close, insisting.

He took the next step, free of burdens.

❖ ❖ ❖

One week later

The SteenCo Kid wasn't so smug now. He was back at The Eat. He was standing with Darlus and Tector. Darlus punched a button and put down the SteenCo sat phone. "The company says we got to go in there and find Old Mose. They say you're coming with us."

Stephen Hillard lives with his wife, Sharmaine, in Grand Junction, Colorado. He is an attorney, private

equity entrepreneur, sometimes author and infrequent television producer.

In 2018, Stephen and Grand Junction native Dennis Nowlan authored a comic book entitled Farway Canyon (available from comixology.com and ka-blam.com). Set in the canyon lands of western Colorado, it is currently in development as a TV series by director Anthony Ferrante (Sharknado I - VI).

The story of Old Mose and the Mill, told here, is a previously unexplored spin-off from the larger world introduced in the comic book. Interestingly, the Mill is based closely on the original Climax Uranium Mill in Grand Junction.

CLARENCE CECILIA'S REST HOME FOR VAMPIRES
by Rose Kite

Medicare Guidelines: Section V, Subset 3.

ICD9; V90.91 Diagnosis: Terminal Hemodesidero (Vampirism).

Admission guidelines: Admission is based on a prior diagnosis of Hemodesidero, with new presentation of reflection cast in mirror. Reflection, coupled with prior diagnosis, assures terminal condition and thus admission.

"Eh," I said with jerk of chin at Rodrigo, home maintenance and all-around-staff person, when he hauled big rough-cut black oak coffin in earlier this evening. "Whose is coffin?"

I got usual response from Rodrigo, shrug of shoulders and big toothy smile. I had yet to hear him speak. So, I hung in great anticipation from my favorite perch at hallway intersection of Clarence Cecilia's Rest Home for Vampires. Where the coffin goes, there goes the vampire, so they say. There would be arrival soon. I wondered who was coming.

"*Incoming, incoming,*" squawked the hand-held on night nurse's desk. Val, the nurse, startled, grabbed the radio and stuffed it into her pocket as she hurried to admissions area. Clarence Cecilia's outer door banged open so hard it hit the wall with a big thud. In strode great, burly figure. In bat form, I viewed upside-down apparition.

Val raised holy water spritzer in alarm as she viewed this giant. Alaric's long hair, held back by headband, swayed with him as he lumbered from side to side down hall. Knee-high wolfskin boots tracked muddy footprints along the tile floor. His cape, the skin of great brown bear, left muddy trail of twigs and leaves. Alaric had been having trouble with his shapeshifting even then, and in landing he had taken tumble.

Val motioned for him to step before admission mirror, and placed holy water spritzer and crucifix within close reach while she processed him. He shrugged his bearskin cape to the floor, then stood and stared back at his reflection in the mirror.

I restrained myself until admission was complete before shapeshifting back to vampire form. With deft flip, I landed on my feet. "Alaric?" I said uncertainly. I could not yet believe my eyes.

He paused, look of startlement on his face, then roared, "Sliva? It is you?"

"It is! It is I, Sliva!" I said. We circled each other unbelievingly a couple of times before he grabbed me in great big bear hug. We whooped and hugged with astounded joy. Alaric was like moonlight shining through stormy night clouds to me. We had not seen each other since the Magyars left the Ural Mountains.

"Shit," Val said, eyeing the bearskin. "Are you two done? I'm not touching that filthy thing."

After hesitation, with sweeping bow to Val and sly wink to me, Alaric picked up cape. I showed him to his room, which happened to be right across the hall from mine. We left Rodrigo, who had come out of nowhere to sweep up the mess Alaric's arrival had left in admissions area.

Alaric slung his bearskin across bottom of his coffin, and turned to me. Then I showed him around his new home. We stopped first at office near entrance. Agnes, head honcho here, had been waiting to meet the new arrival before she went home for end of her day, which was start of our night. She was young, this Agnes. She stood, smiled, and shook Alaric's hand in welcome. She wore crucifix, but also showed much interest and friendship with us residents of Clarence Cecilia's. I helped Agnes schmooze with public by allowing myself and coffin to be used on tours. I only did this because I liked Agnes. She had explained how the tours helped the public see vampires as people, which would help to obtain necessary funding to keep the doors open.

We watched her turn and wave to us after she'd punched code in and left through entrance doors. Then we talked as we strolled halls.

"You were not one I expected to see here," Alaric said as we wove our way around other ambling night denizens on the gleaming pale-tiled floors. The light-filled hallways surrounded us as we strode past night-filled windows.

"A Home or the Stake," I said to Alaric, who nodded slowly. That was the motto Adult Protective Services had put out when it was determined vampires were humans with an eventually terminal chronic illness. Of course there were other symptoms: decrease in stamina, insomnia, dementia, inability to shapeshift, but reflection cast in mirror almost always resulted in final death within six months.

Clarence Cecilia's Rest Home for Vampires resembled most old persons' homes. Head honcho's office and assistants were on either side of one long hallway at entrance. This hallway intersected with another long hallway. At the intersection sat the nurses' station. One difference: beside the red-tanked fire extinguishers were white-tanked sprayers with red crosses. These were holy water dispensers in case of a vampire revolt. They had never been used.

The dining room sat at the end of one of the hallways. There, the resemblance to a regular nursing home ended, for at the end of the other hallway rose a great eight-story glass atrium. I had saved best for last to show Alaric. Spacious Activity Room, with domed ceiling of clear glass (safety, of course—an OSHA requirement), was favorite spot of every resident. Arms folded in front of him, gleaming black tiles below, Alaric lifted his face to the star-filled night sky and smiled. I felt relief, that maybe Alaric could be happy here after all.

We went back to dining room and sat at assigned table with others, tablecloth and napkins in place. Alaric had arrived at dinner time. Images flashed through my mind. I recalled that coppery taste in my mouth as I glanced at Alaric. I knew what that questioning look from him meant. Clarence Cecilia's Rest Home for Vampires, located in Elkhart, Kansas, had sounded like intriguing place to me. Elkhart *was* nice little town, but to my disappointment, there were no elk. Dreams of flying through night sky to pounce on back of fleeing beasts, blood flowing past my fangs, remained just that: dreams. I explained to Alaric how we were civilized vampires now, with manners. Alaric took sip from glass placed in front of him and spit it out, coughing.

"You will get used to it," I whispered. Alaric looked at me with blank stare.

All the vampires in dining room, we looked around at each other guiltily. Alaric expressed what we all felt. Mealtimes were disappointment. When society decided to help us, years of research had been done to create a genetically enhanced artificial polymer to replace blood. Its name consisted of yo-yo string of syllables, so long that when supplement was released, society rolled it up into something that more easily slid off tongue: Vitamin V. V was vital to nourish and sustain us. But V lacked...tang of life? There was no warm, pulsing, metallic taste as it flowed over our tongues. We sat and sipped and tolerated. There was nothing so sad as that

lonely glass of V sitting in front of you, while across
dining room table, senile old Zoran gummed his rolled-
up napkin with denture fangs, reminding us all of what
we had lost to be here.

Alaric and I had met eons ago, shortly after I'd dug
my way out of my burial ground. Woman can only
mourn for so long, and I had mourned my dead husband
beside me for an age or two. Stirring from beside his
crumbled skeleton, I clawed my way past bones of his
favorite horse. With broken, dirt-caked nails, I
burrowed through scattered pottery shards left from
food pots placed in grave for our journey to land of
dead—journey I had yet to take. I burst from the ground
famished and furious. Furious that I had not been able
to die, that my bones had not crumbled to dust next to
those of my husband.

Beyond dim candlelight shining through window of
small hut in wood, I circled in surrounding darkness for
human prey. Weave of garlic hung over door. In silence,
I waited for some unwary soul to come out. Dawn
approached, and man opened door to come outside to
feed oxen. I crept closer. Sudden tackle from side bowled
me over. Alaric, who had been watching, knocked me to
ground and prevented my attack on human. The
frightened farmer ran back inside, slammed and bolted
door.

Alaric helped me up and brushed me off. I looked up
at mountain of vampire, dressed in clothing that spoke of

far north country. Something of him, also, spoke of much older times. He rumbled to me in chiding voice, "We do not have to become the demons they think we are. I will show you the way. I will show you how we sup on those who are already dying." He raised a finger and added, "If you are to come with me, never, never do we prey on children."

That night, when moans and mutterings of dying on some unknown battlefield pierced silence of darkness, we took nourishment from those with mortal wounds.

I found a man lying unconscious, far gone into oozing gut wound. As I bent over him, suddenly he opened his eyes.

"Art thou the angel of mercy?" he asked in wonder.

"I am this night," I replied in echoing wonder as I took him.

After we feasted, Alaric sprang to his feet, threw his head back, and roared, "Which do you want, arms or wings?" And in an instant, in bat form, he lifted off. I followed. We streaked skyward, darting and flitting around each other. We soared beneath star-speckled vault, framed by distant mountain ranges bordering flat steppes. From thousands of feet high, he changed back to human form and dropped in steep dive. His great bear cape rippled. At last minute, back to bat he changed, hovering for a moment before shifting back to vampire and dropping to earth.

We haunted battlefields through centuries. Alaric and I took only those who were at death's door and thus too far gone to become vampires themselves. That was curse we would not bestow on others. This hunting felt righteous. We eased the suffering of the dying. We were dark angels.

This is something learned through ages of vampire's life: as long as mankind is on earth, there will be no lack of wars, no shortage of victims on verge of death.

In a few weeks, Alaric was more like the old Alaric I had known. I often saw him sitting in front of television in central hallway. He was like me, fascinated with the Weather Channel. Not for us, reality shows. We had lived more reality than anyone living could experience. I saw Agnes, head honcho, had won him over. He was gesturing and explaining something to her with smile that made her laugh.

Agnes then turned to me as I approached. "Are you up for another tour tomorrow evening?" I, vampire schmoozer, agreed. Agnes, oh so carefully, allowed public to glimpse a bit of our shadow world.

Next evening I heard Agnes through lid of coffin. That was signal to me that the time was close to sunset and tour would be starting. "How many of you thought vampires were immortal?" I heard Agnes ask. "Yes, I know you're thinking of the wooden stake through the heart thing, and there *is* that, but I'm talking about a natural death." Agnes gave light tap on lid, then I heard her voice fading as she led the tour out of my room. Knock on coffin was my signal they would be back soon. I quickly rose from my coffin to get ready to greet them when tour came back to my room. On not-tour evenings I would wear bathroom slippers and silky pajamas, my hair in snarls and knots. Tonight I donned my long dark gown, the one sheared thin by night winds and flying. I brushed my hair long and flowing down my back.

When Agnes returned with the tour group, Alaric had joined me to greet them. Agnes smiled at him and thanked him for wanting to join in. We politely nodded and shook hands with those who dared. There are rules. In all vampire rest homes, no hissing and no fang showing was allowed. But for Agnes, just for show, I bared small polite fang. Everyone liked little fright, Agnes had told me. It would help with funding. Tour group gasped then tittered. I pretended baring fang was accident and apologized. I slipped fang back in and smiled apology smile, like stupid vampire.

Alaric gave a courtly old-world bow and smiled broadly. Agnes gave a slight nod and smiled back. We had done well again.

Agnes made time to visit me and Alaric a lot. She appeared genuinely interested in all we had seen. Times we had lived through fascinated her. I told her of sacking of Rome, from rooftop watching pillaging Goths as they stormed streets, Romans running before them. I told her of times before Renaissance when societies were just forming. I spoke of Black Death and how it emptied cities. I did not tell her how that blood tasted, how its taint was almost unpalatable.

Agnes and I sometimes talked of our childhoods. I told her I was born into tribe so ancient it had been forgotten. She told me she grew up here in Elkhart, Kansas, part of Wilson tribe. We talked of many things and of nothings. She told me macaroni and cheese was on sale two boxes for three dollars and that her boy, Johnny, was now into size seven slim jeans. I spoke of milking mares for morning meals, and treasures my husband had given me—honey-colored amber necklace, hammered gold armlet. I told her of our music, which I missed more than anything. I described plunking sounds of morin khuur, horsehead fiddle. I told her of time when I had skulked in shadows beyond flames of campfire out on cold, high steppe, beneath moon-flooded sky full of scudding clouds. I had been drawn in by scent of some tempting slant-eyed, honey-skinned boy, alone except for his horse. The unknown words he crooned to plunking stringed melody had so moved me, I closed my eyes and swayed like cobra. My feelings rose within me like the sparks from the fire that flowed up into night sky. I told Agnes he was another I had not touched. I had turned and left hungry. She smiled and patted my hand.

I did not think she would remember that story, but Agnes came back the next evening with her phone. Wondrous plunking sounds of horsehead fiddle filled the air and woke me. I thought there were probably not many head honchos like Agnes.

I must admit, having Alaric here had livened place up. Bingo afternoons, in Activity Room, I looked forward to him roaring "BINGO!" and pounding table with his fist. Minor revolution occurred when staff had audacity to verify his bingo, while he sniffed in pretend belligerence.

At first, staff was afraid of Alaric. I hooted with laughter. Once they got to know kindness and teasing in him, they laughed with him too.

Winter was long, long darkness, which we liked. The winds moaned and gusted at our windows. We played bingo to snow pellets tapping at skylight, and danced Zumba to rackety, drumming music in domed Activity Room.

Then spring came and Zoran died. We all knew how much he had been suffering for very long time. He had not known anyone for months. Still, his death stirred us all. He was first of residents to pass since I came here.

When he failed to rise, Zoran's coffin was opened. His denture fangs were the only things remaining among his ashes.

That spring night, beneath moon obscured by thin clouds, we scattered his ashes in garden where only moon flowers grow. Moon flowers are story of us: closed tight during day, white blooms opening with night. Now when we took our nocturnal strolls, the air would be filled with moon flower scent and we would think of Zoran. We were all despondent with passing of Zoran. His death brought home to us reality of our dying.

Flight night tonight! A bulletin board posted with black bats and colorful letters announced it. Best of all, Rodrigo would be playing his accordion.

I arose that evening and donned my dark flight gown. Hurriedly I ran a brush through my hair and stepped out of my room, to see the back of Alaric as he strode down hallway, great bear cape flaring behind him. He, most of all, had been anticipating tonight.

Best flight nights were with Rodrigo, when he played his accordion. He came, shorts and sandals always. He sat spraddle-legged, accordion on his lap, as his fingers, quick like mice, scurried up and down keyboard. Always, huge smile he had. Big-bellied, hairy-legged, Rodrigo silently swayed back and forth, squeezing instrument into some mad old melody.

As we passed through doorway into Activity Room, Rodrigo's melody engulfed us, and we shapeshifted into bats. Lifting into the air, higher and higher we soared, Alaric ahead of us all. We swerved and swooped, diving at each other in ancient glee, our shadows casting a flickering lunar dance upon gleaming tile floor.

We flew for hours until Rodrigo took break. We all shapeshifted back and surrounded V punch bowl and supped. Our spirits had been lifted, and our conversations were of old nights and old flights.

When Rodrigo returned and took up his accordion, his fingers played out a few lilting notes. We all swayed in anticipation. Then he sprang into a frenetic tune that had us all antsy to fly. One by one we began to shapeshift and lift off. When Alaric tried to shapeshift, his attempt was like strobing light as he fluttered back and forth from bat to vampire. Finally, he found bat form, and he flew at safety glass that separated us from night sky. He charged it again and again until finally he fluttered to floor, changing once more to final vampire form.

The rest of that night he spent glowering, sitting along wall as we flew above him. Rodrigo kept playing, but he had lost his smile and gave sad shake of his head.

After that, Alaric no longer strode halls. He shambled. He was withdrawn and no longer did he smile. This was how he had been since last flight evening with Rodrigo. From that time on, Alaric could no longer shapeshift. He remained in human form and started having trouble with falling. He had to resort to walker, one of those with lime-green tennis balls on hind legs. He slowly shuffled up and down halls, with such pain and misery on his face all the time I thought he looked as though he had been impaled.

A pall descended upon us. We no longer paced the halls and nodded politely. We stalked and snarled. Staff nervously clutched holy water spritzers close to them.

Summer arrived in Elkhart, Kansas with stifling heat. Air conditioning did not reach inside our coffins. We sweltered in them. Days slid into nights and we yearned for cooler weather. V arrived and was dispensed. Shifts came on and shifts clocked out. Val was tolerated. We woke and rose, night after night. New soils replaced old for those who had accidents in their coffins. We had all been in fog of depression and fugue for long time.

Mid-July came. The heat had been unrelenting for weeks. One late afternoon, I awoke and pushed my coffin lid aside. The time was earlier than I expected. Remaining light was dim, as sun was hidden behind low curtain of sullen clouds. In queer late-afternoon light, I saw sky had turned roiling, dirty green. As I entered hall from my room, spatter of raindrops hit sidewalk in front and streaked down windows. The wind came in rising gusts.

Tornado sirens started wailing. The staff all spread out to implement disaster instructions. They started herding the residents who had already risen back into their coffins. There was much shouting and clatter. In this hubbub, Agnes came running up sidewalk, shoulders hunched and notebook over her head in slanting rain and wind. She hurried in door, swinging it wide, and strode down hall.

In all this hurry I noticed Alaric with his walker. Moving slowly but determinedly, he was heading to entrance door Agnes had just come through. Alaric looked up as he moved past me. I could see thought in his eyes. Escape lit his glance. I could also see he wasn't going to make it to door in time before it shut and locked. Right code had to be punched into keypad beside door for door to open.

I knew something. I was schmoozer. I was one staff trusted. I possessed secret. Staff had been careless when

I was close, and I had seen numbers they punched in. I knew code.

In an instant, much went through my mind. Memories of Alaric's many kindnesses, his noble gestures, but especially his passion for flight—which he would never do again—flashed before me. I shapeshifted and flew to door and shapeshifted back when I landed. I punched in code, and door slowly opened. In all this alarm, Alaric was going to get away—and I was going with him. I gave a thought to how we must look: aging Romeo and Juliet trying to escape from warring families. But we were not. We were just two old vampires trying to get away from this thing that pursued all of humanity. We were choosing to meet it on our own terms: face to face, snout to snout.

Alaric reached door and tottered outside, his walker bumping across threshold. I was right behind him. A cold, wet wind lashed our faces. In corner of my eye I saw we had been spotted. Val was running to stop us. I turned and looked. Alaric was only a few feet down sidewalk.

I saw twister in the distance over Elkhart. It was snaking down from low swirling storm clouds. Twister was flimsy little F1, F2 wannabe, and couldn't keep its tail on ground. It kept dipping and lifting, skipping across town. Spiraling debris filled the air around it.

I saw Alaric wouldn't make it in time. I could shapeshift and be gone in an instant. He couldn't. He would be caught by Val and pulled back inside, to spend the rest of his life miserably shambling down hallways.

I stopped and turned around and slipped back inside. I pulled door shut. Val raced toward me.

I prepared to make my stand in front of door. I inhaled and raised myself upright. I arced my arms overhead, crouched, and bared my fangs. I hissed and snarled and hissed and snarled. Val backpedaled so fast she tripped with her duck shoes and fell on her well-cushioned bottom, her stethoscope clattered to one side, and her name tag flew off. She quickly regained her feet, though. She lifted holy water spritzer from her belt and aimed. Then evil smile crossed her face. She dropped her spritzer, strode to wall, and pulled holy water extinguisher down.

I stood there in front of door, hissing and fanging with looks over my shoulder as I kept track of Alaric's progress through the window of the entrance door. The tornado was coming right down street now in its erratic journey. It had passed through some vacant lots, and it had picked up dancing skirt of dirt, debris, and tumbleweeds.

As roaring wind drowned out wail of sirens, I glanced at Val and cringed. I looked back at Alaric, still moving toward twister. Lime-green tennis balls on back legs of his walker stood out in dim light of approaching storm.

Then it was upon him. He disappeared into swirling dust.

Val strode toward me, and I prepared to be burned by holy water. I cringed.

Suddenly a figure rushed at me from side. It was Rodrigo. With spread legs, he planted himself in front of me, facing Val. He stretched a palm out, and a thundering "No!" came out of him. Val skidded to a halt.

In stalemate, I glanced outside. There was no trace of Alaric. Only his walker lay where the tornado had tumbled it up on the front lawn. Lime-green tennis balls were missing.

"I'm going to fill out an incident report, and you are going to be in so much trouble," Val said to me as Rodrigo took the holy water extinguisher from her.

Glad-sad, I went into Alaric's room and looked at his absence. There was his open coffin. I climbed in and closed the lid down over me. In dark, I lay back in depressions he made in his soil and breathed deeply. The smell of Alaric surrounded me. I closed my eyes and thought of the nights we flew through star-filled skies, both of us roaring. The silence of him gone was deafening.

A knock on lid. Agnes's voice said, "We have to talk." A long pause, then, "Tomorrow night will be okay." A fumbling sound as something was placed on coffin lid, and the sounds of morin khuur filled room. I heard the fading sound of Agnes's heels clicking out of room.

As I listened to strumming melody, some ancient song from way-gone times, my thoughts were of Alaric. In my mind's eye I saw him confronting tornado. I saw him swirling and circling, being pulled ever higher in tornado's rotation. I imagined him as he soared out into full rays of last sunlight of day. He would have been surrounded by light as he burned to cinders, as he flew one last time.

Within the darkness, I smiled.

Rose Kite is the pen name for this Western Slope writer of fantasy and science fiction. She also writes historical fiction under the name C. J. Gruenewald. Her roots run deep in Colorado history, which is the wellspring of her inspiration. She grew up on Eastern Colorado ground, farmed and ranched by her great-great-grandparents. The airy plain, the overlooked part of Colorado, forms the basis of many of her stories.